VARICK

The Borden Years

JOHN GONZALES

First Edition

PAGE PUBLISHING
Conneaut Lake, PA

First originally published by Page Publishing 2022

ISBN 978-1-6624-7541-2 (pbk)
ISBN 978-1-6624-7542-9 (digital)

Printed in the United States of America

CHAPTER 1

Epiphany

A nocturnal orchestra of crickets akin to a million violins was fading slowly in the background with the setting moon as the night came to a close. Dwindling moonbeams radiated above a foreboding landscape, unable to infiltrate the dark crevices that marked the area in various shades of black. Varick hunkered down on a thick branch of a tamarack tree at the edge of a bog with a hand resting on its trunk. It was well past midnight, and he hadn't found a thing to eat yet. Many of the nocturnal creatures roaming about were too small and insufficient to satisfy his appetite. His hunger would require a large animal, which was usually found out and about in the daylight hours. *Feeding used to be much easier*, he thought with frustration, while he scanned the scenery and softly inhaled the air for any hint of warm blood.

The soles of his monkey boots were wearing thin, and he could feel the knots and twists of the tree branch pushing into the arches of his feet. He adjusted his balance and straightened out the lapels of his maroon leather coat and smoothed the collar of his shirt. *There may be food out there,* he pondered as he viewed the edge of the brush where the bog finished. But was there enough time to travel there, locate food, and make it back to their shelter without risking his safety? Looking up at the half-moon to estimate how much time he had before sunrise, his hunger decided for him, and off he went.

It was worth the risk. Varick located a group of white-tailed deer sleeping under an immense briar patch with thorns two inches long within minutes after leaving the bog. It was a young mother with two calves. Each slept peacefully under the protection of their thorny inn. He could smell their blood with each breath that exhaled from their wet noses as they slumbered. He stretched his body out on the ground and crawled under the patch like an alligator. In complete silence, he inched toward the mother, grabbed her by the muzzle, and held it shut tight with one hand while he held her body down with the other and began to feed slowly, making sure not to wake the kids.

On his return to the swamp where he and Henry were currently taking a respite from any sort of encounter with anyone or anything because of the grief suffered from their last misadventure, Varick sensed unwanted activity from different directions. He could smell rotting flesh coming from the west, so he had no doubt as to what was approaching, but there were other sounds: whispers and breaking twigs that were much closer. Humans. Live, healthy ones. He wiped his tongue across his top row of teeth, rubbing it around the tip of his extended canine, and thought about an after-supper snack of some real blood. But when he looked up at the brightening sky, he decided it would be better to return to the grotto.

He landed with the lightness of a butterfly at the entrance of the hideaway and crept his way along the wall of roots until he was behind Henry, who was facing the entrance and admiring his machete and whistling a familiar melody. Varick smiled internally when he realized what it was: "Lizzie Borden took an axe..."

*****

Deep within a recess located at the end of a rivulet entirely concealed from all species of passersby with a forest of unbridled mangroves and Spanish moss, a pair of sinewy, bronze-skinned hands were steadily working, applying whetstone to metal. Hands that at one time only knew the feel of a television remote and a morning wood, but were now more comfortable with iron and steel, were filing the edge of a well-used machete with the dexterity and precision of a master forger. Soft crunching sounds resonated from the erasing of blemishes that diminished with each motion. Raising the machete to examine his work, he studied the blade with a furrowed brow of concentration and gave it a look that read, "Something isn't right." Holding the machete in the firmest of grips, protruding knuckles surrounding the handle, he sighed, "I can't let it go. Damn song. I hate it when that happens. 'Lizzie Borden took an axe and gave her mother forty whacks…' Now I'm going to be singing that damn thing all day."

He began to rework the steel, thinking to himself that if he were to focus on the blade, the obnoxious melody will be pushed out of his head. In an instant, an image of overdue earwax dripping from his earlobes and oozing onto his favorite shirt appeared in his mind's eye. "Eeww!"

Forty minutes later, as he moved past the blade of the machete and began cleaning the handle, he thought to himself how out of all the improvised weaponry he has come across, this piece had definitely been the most reliable and durable; if there was a notch on the handle for every kill, it would look like a corncob. A hint of cynical humor touched his eyes as nostalgia swept over him like a cool trade wind. All of a sudden he was short of breath, sweaty, and shitting a brick. Just like the day when he, literally, stumbled upon "old reliable." All the while he was subconsciously whistling the melody of Lizzie Borden.

*****

That day seemed to have no end. The sun grew hotter with each hour, and its glare grew brighter as the temperature rose, limiting the area of vision to within the nearest blinding reflection of light. Shadows never moved, and it felt like it was high noon for at least half of the day, although dusk was just around the corner.

He was alone, again, in a world of constant running where life consists of one goddamned thing after another, being forced to flee from place to place like a frightened dormouse evading a barnyard cat. Crisscrossing through vacant lots and empty properties with desolate, hollow structures encased by years of slow-growing vines, dilapidated tenements whose sole usefulness is providing shelter for rodents and the other feral animals reclaiming their lost land, as well as the occasional derelict too careless or bone-weary to be concerned for their own personal safety.

He had been on the move for nearly three hours running on an empty stomach and a pair of legs that were beginning to turn to jelly. Running through the overgrown brush of what used to be a neatly trimmed lawn of another abandoned house on another abandoned block in another forgotten neighborhood. He badly needed a break. A few yards to his left, there sat a termite-eaten and weather-beaten porch loosely held together by creepers. He dove under it headfirst, scraping his forehead on the way, and faded blue flakes of ancient paint sprinkled his shoulders and back.

For an instant there was quiet, too much quiet. He could hear his droplets of sweat crashing onto the dry leaves below him booming like cannonballs. "Are they still out there? How long can they keep this up?" he stressed to himself. A shooting pain started to make its way along his legs, and his buttocks began to spasm. *Not now*, he thought as his legs stiffened. He shouldn't have stopped moving. The scrape on his scalp began to throb, and a tiny rivulet of blood and sweat began to make its way past his eyebrow.

At that moment, emerging behind the amplified echo of his drumming pulse, he heard the rustle of long grass parting and the crunch of dry vegetation. Here they come. "Don't move. Don't even blink," he told himself. "Just keep your teeth together, and they'll pass." Yet the more he focused on remaining still, the more difficult it became to fight the urge to explode. "Please, God, let them pass?" God flew the coop a long time ago, an inner voice told him. Meanwhile, they drew closer while his legs burned hotter than a cane fire.

Slowly, they moved on as a million heartbeats passed. Eyelids clenched tighter than his ass, he waited. "What's that smell?" Like a child hiding from the boogeyman hoping that Mom is right, and that there really isn't anything living in his closet at night, he cautiously lifted his lids. Staring directly at him was a pair of eyes tensed with danger, one sparking yellow, the other bloodshot and cataract infected. The stench of hot breath penetrated his nostrils as a high-pitched screech pierced his eardrums. A split-second later, he was out from under the porch, standing behind his pursuers, while a raccoon with missing patches of hair fled in the opposite direction.

"*Hijo de la…*" he blurted out unexpectedly. At that moment, hunters and prey simultaneously pulled a one eighty and continued the chase, retracing their previous course. Only this time his flight attempt was put to a stop when his feet became tangled in some trailing weeds, and he tumbled face-first into a thick tuft of crabgrass. As he struggled to get to his feet, his left hand clutched something solid underneath the overgrown foliage. From the shape of it he could tell that it wasn't a tree root, and it wasn't a rock. He dug his fingers deep into the ground and hastily yanked out bunches of grass, roots and all. The sound of heavy footsteps grew closer. "Shit, man. Come on. Curiosity killed that cat," he whispered to himself as he pulled the object out from under the overgrowth with some effort, and a grunt, then rose to his feet. It was a machete about the length of a cattle prod with a one-sided blade like most machetes, except on the blunted side of this one there was a protruding, curved blade akin to a flat fishhook.

It was there and then that he came to an epiphany. "I'm tired of this running shit," he exclaimed. Tightening his grasp around the ornate handle, which strangely resembled the hilt of a sword or gladius, he turned and stalked toward his heavy-footed pursuers with determination on his face and blood on his mind.

Three large strides brought him within striking distance of the unrelenting group. They crept forward, attempting to surround him. Raising the machete to the sky in a flash of fury, he christened the blade and was born again. *Hack, hack, hack.* Every strike landed with complete accuracy as the handle adjusted to his grip perfectly like two beings morphing together as one. It was as if he was destined to discover this hidden jewel beneath Mother Nature's emerald shag carpet.

The leader of the pack went down with ease when the machete hit his skull with a metallic ping that cleansed the blade of leftover caked-on soil. Dirt and blood flew in his face as he removed the blade and swung full force toward his second victim, tearing him open diagonally from collarbone to pelvis. Half a torso slid and hit the floor with a damp thud. A third and a fourth moved in closer for the kill. The nearest took it up the middle with a left uppercut to the chin and fell without a jawbone. He toyed with the next one for a second, treading backward, luring him in for the final strike before removing both arms in single motion. *Swoosh!* Switching the machete to his other hand, he removed its head with a right hook. "And that makes three!" he declared while he kicked the still-standing limbless corpse to the ground. Blood spewing from arm stubs in Fourth of July fashion.

Eight or so stragglers remained, and they continued to move forward, trudging over their colleague's limp bodies. Limbs squished underfoot, and the lead pursuer lost his balance and slipped to the ground, landing with a splash in a pool of wet flesh. A small grin appeared on Henry's face. It was the closest he had come to a smile in a very long time—years, perhaps.

The stragglers gathered themselves together while he created distance between them, making his way to the street. After working his way around a couple of stranded cars with blades of elephant grass sprouting through the headlight caps like false eyelashes, he stopped in the middle of the pavement and waited for them to follow. Leading them down the side street to the main avenue of whatever town he was in he killed them one by one, or two at a time. He couldn't tell anymore.

He finished the last of them with a machete to the eye and pivoted with arms swinging in continuous defensive motions, but there was no one there, nothing except the breeze in the trees. *I survived. I survived another nightmare*, he thought to himself as he stood at the crossroads of the main thoroughfare and the side street he had just emerged from, leaving a trail of dead breadcrumbs for those who desire the same fate. A squeaky hinge squealed to his left. He looked up and saw a rusted street sign swaying gently on its post and burst out in uncontrollable laughter until tears ran down both sides of his face creating streams of dirt. The sign read *Elm Street*.

His maniacal laughter, bordering on wailing, was carried over the air current to ears that perked up with excitement and were immediately drawn toward the commotion. Slowly but surely, deadly appetites began making their way to his location.

Simultaneously, from the safety of an overhanging tree branch, a raccoon with missing patches of hair and one dead eye looked on with curiosity at the noisy two-legged animal as he stomped down the street, laughing at the moon.

*****

His mind returned from the brief walk down memory lane to the present where he was subconsciously working the blade of the machete solely from muscle memory and still whistling the Lizzie Borden tune. “Damnit,” he exclaimed and refocused his attention, with intensity, back to the honing of his weapon.

After working the blade until its edge was razor sharp, he studied the machete for a while, rotating it in his now agile hands, examining the handles intricate metalwork. He wasn’t well versed in history, or art—or anything at all, really—but he did know that the design concept and technique didn’t resemble any of the typical medieval Excalibur kind of stuff he was familiar with from the classic movies he used to watch on his grandma’s black-and-white television.

At first glance, the hilt looked like an average handle worked by the village blacksmith with cross guard, grip, and pommel. But a closer look told a different story and made it obvious that it was much more than that. The contrasts were evident in each portion of the single-cast piece of iron. The guard, for example, was shaped in a way that gave the cross-section the appearance of two intertwined pieces of steel extending outward ending in a fine point. This pattern continued its way down the grip wrapping around the hilt like braided leather until it reached the pommel at the base of the machete. The pommel itself was no ordinary orb simply made to counterweight the machete’s blade. It was styled in the shape of what looked like a snake's head—or possibly a dragon—with large, protruding fangs. The eyes on either side were round and bulging, as well as the nostrils. The serpent's head complimented the intertwining metalwork of the haft and cross guard as the braided metal form also contained etchings that appeared to be scales of a fish, but were actually finely worked overlapping feathers. Plus, the age of the iron piece gave the feathers a turquoise hue when exposed to the sun's ultraviolet rays.

He never expected the design to have any real significance except that it was cool, and that it reminded him of some of the pictures in those free calendars from the *carneceria* that his *abuela* hung in her kitchen. *Damn, I miss my grandma*, he thought to himself, nodding in dismay.

However, it wasn't until Varick told him about what he called the feathered serpent of Meso-America, Quetzalcoatl, that he started to realize the implication of his find given his ancestry, and that it was something very exceptional. It was back when they first met. Who knows when that was? Time seemed to have stopped when all this shit started.

A vision of Varick's emotionless expression popped up in his brain, the one that still creeps him out. He was shuffling the machete back and forth in his eggshell-colored, perpetually manicured hands as he related to me that the reptilian figure was a representation of the Aztec deity, Quetzalcoatl. Known to the Mayans as Kukulcan, the diviner of the Fifth Sun, Lord of the Four Cardinal Directions, and the Father who granted humans the knowledge to create maize, corn. The most notable of the legends, he went on to explain, tells of how Quetzlcoatl, in his human form, was a wise and benevolent ruler who brought prosperity and peace to the world. But his siblings grew jealous and turned the people against him through political intrigue, murder, and lies.

At this point in the story, a tiny smirk tried to escape Varick's stoic expression as he commented on how Shakespearian the tale was, very similar to a Greek tragedy. "Subsequently," he continued, "Quetzalcoatl was exiled, and he departed eastward on a raft crafted of scores of serpents woven together carrying him out to sea. And dramatically, he vowed to return one day to bring peace and prosperity back to the people of Anahuac." When he returned the machete to Henry, Varick glanced at the handle and stated, "An extraordinary find indeed."

*****

With a sigh, Henry looked up to admire what little view their secluded, dank location had to offer. They had been holed up in here for about a week recuperating and licking their wounds; that last encounter was a deadly reminder for Henry that no one can be trusted. No matter how righteous they seemed to be. He could see the dawn's purplish hue making its segue into another sunny day peeking through the forest gaps, and smell the moldy vegetation in the air that was temporarily camouflaging the everyday odor of decay and death. The morning was on the rise once again. *It's getting late*, he thought. "Should I be worried? Nah, he's a big boy. He can take care of himself," he muttered, unaware of the slender figure standing behind him in the darkness of the fading shadows.

"Yes, I am quite capable of taking care of myself."

Henry quickly jumped to his feet, reaching for a wooden spear that lay just a few inches away. In the process his machete dropped to the floor with a clang.

"You scared the crap outta me, man. I thought I asked you not to do that creepy-sneaky thing of yours." Showing up in places and appearing out of thin air was another thing that he just couldn't get used to. "I told you to give me a heads-up, remember? You remember everything else like a damn elephant." He set the spear back down on the floor and picked up the machete, grumbling to himself while he reexamined the blade, looking for blemishes.

"It's in my nature. It cannot be helped. However, I do appreciate the concern. It's quite human of you," Varick quipped.

Henry laughed under his breath at the remark, and he continued to unconsciously whistle the tune to Lizzie Borden. Varick stopped in midstep when he recognized the melody and looked up with his head tilted and eyelids half-closed as if he was trying to catch a familiar whisper.

"Aah…she was a beast, pure unadulterated rage," he breathed.

A moment passed before the weight of his words settled in Henry's brain. "Hmm… Wait, what?" he asked just to be sure he heard correctly.

"Miss Borden," Varick said nonchalantly. "That is the tune you're singing, isn't it? 'Lizzie Borden took an axe and gave her mother forty whacks.' She was definitely thee most dedicated, and brutal, vampire killer of her time. The mere mention of her name caused even the boldest vampires to pause with apprehension. And it was only nineteen whacks," he stated as he turned to walk toward the furthest reach of their temporary dwelling to begin his daily rejuvenation.

Henry stood there for a moment in the still, dank air jaw agape and wide-eyed in wonderment, staring at Varick as he lay motionless, blending with the shadows and offering no further comment other than silence. Yet at the same time there seemed to be this smug look on his face that read, "Hey, you know how to keep a mortal in suspense?"

"Damn him!" he grunted through his teeth. "He does this shit on purpose."

He needed to know. With the clownish stealth of a cartoon character, he tiptoed his way toward Varick and gingerly prodded his rib cage with the end of the spear several times, like a young boy checking to see if the strange lump of fur lying in his backyard was alive or dead.

"Did I just hear you ramble on about Lizzie Borden being a vampire killer?" he asked.

No response. He attempted another jab. But before he could make contact, the spear was taken from his hands and protruding from an ancient tree trunk that supported their hideaway. Iron-rich, cold air brushed his face, and Varick was standing nose to nose with him. His weary, bloodshot, yet still somehow captivating eyes stared him down to the size of an unruly child.

"Sorry!" Henry blurted.

For a moment there was a picture of pure bloodthirsty rage complete with an aura of hellfire emanating from behind Varick as he seemed to plead through pressured speech, "You know I despise having my rest interrupted?"

And then, in a flash it was gone immediately, replaced with a look of parental compassion. "Apology accepted. I understand your restlessness. Especially in light of your affinity for the limerick." This last statement was accompanied by a gleam of arrogance and sarcasm.

"Well…did you know her?" Henry asked impatiently after brushing off the comment. "Come on, man, you can't leave me hangin' like this."

There was a short pause before Varick spoke again, and when he did it was with an expression filled with derision. "In answer to your prodding question, I never had the pleasure of knowing her personally, but I knew of her. However, our paths intertwined from time to time as if our destinies were woven from the same fabric, and there was also that brief encounter where it was impressed upon me that my time in Massachusetts had come to a close." When he finished making this statement, the expression of derision on his face slowly changed to one of empathy.

"Really?"

"Yes. Her and her company of courtesans were making it quite obvious that the Northeastern Seaboard was no longer safe for my kind."

"Courtesans?" Henry asked with a look of confusion.

Without responding, Varick turned his head and contemplated the soft beams of the rising sun visible through the canopy of tree limbs. A delicate crunch echoed distantly behind the chirping crickets and rustling wind. They looked toward each other in acknowledgement.

"The sun is here. I think it's time I rest. Besides, you have work to do."

Henry looked toward the entrance of their hideaway, "How many?" he asked.

"Three, maybe four. There's death as well." he whispered before returning to the shaded recess and shutting his eyes for the day.

Henry approached the ancient timber column, removed the spear, picked up his machete, and headed in the direction of the would-be intruders. After several steps, he paused and turned back toward Varick lying in the darkness. "Rest well. Oh, and you owe me a story," he said as he left with the gait and confidence of a huntsman.

CHAPTER 2

Pest Control

"You think he's alone?" one set of eyes asked. Oily dirty-blond hair fell to the sides of filthy hands shading his eyes from dust and nature.

"Let's wait a minute and see," replied the other while burrowing into his right nostril with an index finger caked with grime. "Where's Joshua?"

"I sent him 'round the flank with Germaine as soon as we spotted that guy walkin' 'round," said the oily-haired one.

"Someone's coming," the nose digger whispered with force while he pulled his finger away from his face and reached for a hand-held axe he kept at his side.

The two bodies slunk lower into the brush and waited. A few seconds later a thin figure with a short, unkempt reddish-brown afro emerged from the brush squatting, trying to remain out of sight. His afro puffed out on the sides as if he were recently wearing a baseball cap. He sported a raincoat—the type of raincoat Detective Marlowe would wear, only soiled and shredded along the cuffs and collar, and where there was once a waist belt there was now a braided rope of animal hair. In one hand he held a World War II-era M-1 rifle and in the other a faded green baseball cap.

"Hey, it's me, Trace," the newcomer hailed.

The two watchers revealed themselves from hiding as the newcomer explained, "I was down by the stream, and I could hear another person's voice in there. I couldn't hear what they were talkin' about, but I could hear 'em."

"So he ain't alone," said the nose picker.

"You think they have any food?" asked the dirty blonde in a hushed tone.

"I pray to God they do," said Trace. "I'm starvin' like Marvin, and there ain't no sign of anything to eat out here. Not even a bullfrog."

Greg turned his attention to Curtis. "What's the plan?" he asked.

The nose picker stared at the dank, dark entrance where the tall, thin man had previously disappeared, contemplating. "Let's meet up with Germaine and Josh, and we'll figure it out. We know there's at least two of them, but there may be more. Not too many, though," he stated this more to himself as if thinking out loud. "Let's go."

The trio moved with extreme caution toward the area where their two companions would be waiting for them, unaware that their entire conversation was overheard by a predator in wait who was, at the moment, calculating every movement of the men and deciding how to rid the area of these pests who interrupted his morning. Unfortunately, these days other humans are by and large desperate, deranged pests, and an encounter with most survivors is guaranteed to result in pain or death.

*****

"You got any water?"

"Nope," Joshua quickly replied.

"How long do we wait here?" Germaine impatiently asked. "What are we supposed to be doing anyways?"

"It won't be long. Keep calm," Joshua said while he watched the bog in front of him for any sign of movement. Uneven brown hair, almost black from lack of bathing, sprouted from the top of his head like spikey sea urchins, and the sides and back were marked with nicks and scrapes as a result of many a self-administered haircut. He wore a faded brown long-sleeved T-shirt under a pair of denim overalls that were held together at the seams with rawhide strips. But his boots were in good condition and the envy of the group ever since he took them off a dead man who happened to be living prior to their encounter. In fact, he often referred to them as "Deadman's" as if they were an exclusive brand of footwear. The soles still had treading, and the leather was intact.

A low rumble arose from his right. Germaine was staring at his stomach, rubbing counterclockwise. His round, pale cheekbones blushed, giving the appearance of two red apples planted on his face. He had the look of a teenager who couldn't quite grow a beard or mustache yet, although he was well into his thirties.

"Sorry, man."

"We're' all hungry," Josh exclaimed while concentrating on the landscape, searching for activity.

Just as he thought, he saw something and heard a low *psst* coming from a group of young mangroves huddled together with their roots intertwined like overlapping spider legs piercing into the marshy ground. The mangroves were to the east of him, the direction he would be expecting the rest of his companions to be approaching from.

"Here they come, finally," Germaine said.

Joshua rose to his feet to greet the figure emerging from the mangroves. The rays of the rising sun piercing through the gaps in the forest temporarily blinded him as he raised his hand to shade his eyes. But before his vision cleared, he heard Germaine yell something incoherent just as the man before him grabbed him behind the neck and bore the head of a spear through his right eye until the tip poked through the back of his skull.

Henry removed the spear, and Joshua dropped to the floor like a wet suit. Germaine was on one knee, motionless, eyes darting back and forth from Henry to the rusty, sawed-off shotgun he carelessly left out of his reach. Henry took a knee so that he was level with Germaine's pubescent face.

"How many?" he asked.

"Wha…what?" Germaine stumbled. "I don't know."

A machete with an extremely sharp blade was pressed against Germaine's round cheeks above the bone and just under the eye.

He tried to speak, but all that came out was spittle and drool. Blood began to appear under his eye where the machete met his skin. Henry gripped his throat and asked him again, "How many?"

"Three! There's three more of us!" Germaine blurted.

"I'm not asking about the ones you came with. How many more will miss you when you do not return?" grunted Henry.

Germaine's eyes grew even wider at this question. "It's only us," he replied, shaking his head nervously. Henry thanked him, put the machete to his throat, and slowly sliced his neck open horizontally while the word "Please" screeched from Germaine's lips like an unoiled door hinge.

Now for the others, he thought to himself as he looked down at Germaine's limp body. Deep, hollow moans could be heard far off in the background, reminding him that he needed to finish the job here first. He rested a knee on Germaine's chest and reached down and grabbed a tuft of his mangy hair, lifting him up by the head. He stared at it for a minute, and then the eyelids popped open, eyeballs moving around like loose marbles searching for a victim, while the mouth began to snap and bite. Germaine's dead body started to fight the restraint of Henry's weight bucking like a wild bronco. He pulled out a folding knife he kept in the small of his back and set the tip of the blade at the base of the revitalized Germaine's skull and pushed. The iron grip of the arms that were reaching for his neck slipped away.

*****

Greg treaded silently, carefully stepping over tree roots and avoiding muddy sink holes as best as he could in the limited light while Curtis and Fred followed closely behind. A tree branch cracked loudly, and Greg glanced over his shoulder and gave Curtis an impatient look. "At least try to be quiet," he stressed impatiently. Curtis shrugged his shoulders and offered him an apologetic expression then looked behind him toward Trace as if he was to blame. Greg gave a hand signal, and the three cautiously took a knee several yards away from where they were to rendezvous with their companions.

A plan was hatched for Curtis to retrieve the other two and meet up with Fred and Greg at the entrance of the hideaway within ten minutes or so. The only one of them who had a watch was Greg. It was a wind-up pocket watch on a silver chain he looted from an antique store just when everything went south, and the world turned upside down. A quick memory flashed before him as he stared at the face of the watch: windows smashing and fire hydrants exploding while car alarms and police sirens were crowding the air with the screams of the helpless. He was one of the helpless before the dead arrived, living among the homeless on the sidewalks and in the alleyways of a hip metropolis whose leaders ignored the working class decades before. Yet now was not the time for reflection, and the approaching low, deep groans reminded him that their time was limited here.

"We need to act fast they're getting closer," Greg whispered, looking in the direction of the oncoming commotion. He put the watch in the pocket of his worn pants, gave the signal to move, and the three parted ways. Greg and Fred headed toward a mangrove patch encased in kudzu vines just in front of the entryway to their supposed destination, and Curtis went to fetch Germaine and Josh. All crouching low as to keep out of sight, not realizing their clumsy rambling exposed them to anyone within earshot.

*****

Curtis moved the leafage from his view and called out to Joshua and Germaine, "Hey," but there was no response. The rising sunlight offered a dim view of the area as he searched the spot where they should have been waiting. Maybe they moved farther back to conceal themselves, he thought. He took a few careful steps forward and called out again, "Hey!" Still no response.

"Where are you guys?" he whispered with a hint of worry in his voice.

He spotted movement in the bushes in front of him. "Come on, you guys. We gotta go. Greg's waiting!" he stressed as he walked into the group of bushes. The forest opened up as he treaded through, and it exposed two bodies piled on top of each other with limbs blood-soaked and tangled. "Holy shit!" he screamed in terror and turned to flee the scene, only to come face-to-face with a set of fierce brown eyes staring straight at him. "Hola," a voice breathed and then there was darkness. Curtis could hear himself choking on his own blood and feel the force of metal chopping at his neck.

Henry wiped his machete clean on Curtis's oily hair and rose to his feet. The groans of death were getting closer. He grunted to himself and streamlined it for the last two pests, leaving behind a pile of three dead bodies. One of them missing a head.

*****

"Where are those idiots? They should be here already. These guys aren't gonna stay put for much longer. We gotta move now." Greg and Trace were stooped uncomfortably behind the kudzu-covered mangroves.

"Hold on a second. They ain't got a watch, remember.?" Trace exclaimed, hoping to calm Greg down. He was getting jumpier by the minute. But it was taking them a little longer than usual, Trace thought. And Curtis ain't one to straggle. Maybe they should go and check things out? Greg was right, though. There wasn't much time left. Whatever was in that hideout must be gotten now. They were tired and starving, and those damn demons were getting closer.

Both men were getting fidgety and wanted to act when a familiar whistle blew from the foliage to the right. Greg emerged from the mangroves to greet his fellow scavengers and saw no one. The whistle sounded again, this time from the left. Fred stood up anxiously, aiming his M-1 rifle this way and that, when something heavy landed in front of them with a squish. They darted their eyes toward the swampy floor and found themselves looking at Curtis's muddied and bloodied decapitated head, eyes blinking and full of life while its tongue tossed around, savoring the air.

"What the—" Greg never finished his statement. A spear appeared in the center of his torso, and blood started to bubble out from the gash as it expanded from the dragging weight of the sturdy weapon—his left hand clenching a silver pocket watch. Trace never saw who or where the spear came from, but he was no one's fool, especially now that Greg was dangling from a seven-foot spear. He hightailed it out of there faster than a freight train without looking back. Screaming at the top of his lungs along the way while saplings and dry tree branches smacked him in the face for his rude volume, he forgot to take notice of the direction he was heading.

Meanwhile, Henry steadily stalked Trace through the swampy forest, making sure to steer clear of the approaching problem. Unfortunately, for the past few minutes, Trace continued to run straight toward the unruly commotion. He had to act fast to be able return to the grotto, wake Varick, pack up their belongings, and have enough time to make a somewhat clean getaway before they were overrun. It was going to be a tight squeeze, he admitted to himself. Unless he could do something to buy them a little time.

"Shit!" Trace stubbed his toe on a hidden mangrove root, lost his balance, and slammed into a tree as thick as a telephone pole. He desperately hugged the tree for support. He was spent, heart pounding from fear and exhaustion, and legs ready to collapse. He looked around frantically, but then realized he didn't know what he was searching for. He fled so quickly, he never got sight of what he was running from. He squatted down as low as his unsteady legs would allow him and peered deep into the forest, searching the broken sunlight for movement of any kind.

Thwap! A spear landed in the tree he was leaning on, close enough to graze his neck. He began to scream again and fell back, put his hand to his neck, turned on his belly, and crawled away before rising to run. Henry followed him closely, guiding him with each spear shot to make sure that he moved eastward of the hungry parade, yet still close enough to attract its interest. Each shot missing by a hair's breadth.

"Stop screaming like a little bitch! You can do this!" Trace whispered to himself, panting like an overworked dog as he paused for breath. *Get a hold of yourself,* he thought. *There might only be one person chasing me.* He took a chance to peek around the half-dead tree stump he was using for cover, and a knife pierced the hand resting against the rotting wood, removing an index finger. "Aahhh!" The sound poured from Trace's mouth with the force of a tsunami and could be heard from far and wide. A half-mile to the west, the sound was caught echoing in the damp morning air, and hungry eyes shifted direction to investigate its origin.

As Trace pulled his hand away from the tree, leaving the knife and his finger behind, a dark shadow approached him from the surrounding forest. "Aahhh!" he screamed again and took off running eastward, just as Henry expected. If all worked out as planned, the pest would reach the clearing and take the parade of death with him. He followed Trace to the edge of the forest and launched another spear shot to make sure that the parade followed him. The spear appeared in one of the trees at the forest's edge just next to Trace, which was followed by another scream as he fled out into the stretch of plain between the highway and the swampland.

Henry observed from the concealing forest as Trace ran across the plain, screaming at the top of his lungs, leaving his old baseball cap in the dust. Henry shifted his gaze to the left and could see the long grass of the clearing parting as the parade of decayed hunters stalked their terrified prey. Trace looked back and spotted the deathly crowd hot on his heels. A distant scream was heard, and then Trace disappeared into the warm horizon accompanied by his new friends.

Along the way back to the temporary abode, Henry stopped to retrieve his knife from the tree stump, allowing Trace's finger stub to drop in a pile of composting leaves. The sun was shining brightly, peering through the blotchy patchwork of the forest when he reached his destination. As he approached the entrance, a wailing moan called to him from behind a familiar group of mangroves. Henry followed the noise around the bunch of interlaced trees and standing there trying to pull his leg out from an uncomfortable situation was Greg, with his chin resting against his chest while blood dripped from his drooping head.

"Shit," he declared, shaking his head with a light smile on his face, "I almost forgot about that one." Resurrected, Greg looked up at the sound of Henry's voice and tried to walk toward him in a desperate attempt at capturing him for a bite to eat with hands flailing, one clenching a silver stopwatch. Unfortunately, for Greg, his foot was lodged between a set of tree roots and prevented him from moving. Henry sidled up next to Greg, cautiously approaching from the rear, as to not allow Greg to get a hold of him and slowly inserted the knife into the base of his neck where the spine meets the skull. Greg offered resistance at first, jerking his head from left to right like a mad dog trying to get a nip at Henry, before the former grabbed Greg's mangy scalp to steady him. The knife went in with some effort until Greg's snapping jaw ceased. Henry leaned Greg's body against a nearby tree and cleaned the blood and filth on his old trousers. He was about to walk away when he saw something shining through the fingers of Greg's death grip. He forced his fingers open and caught the watch before it fell to the floor. When he saw what it was, he whistled softly and rubbed its face clean before putting it in his back pocket, leaving its chain dangling.

It was midmorning when Henry neared the entrance to the hideaway, and he could see through the forest gaps that the sun was reaching its peak. It was going to be a hot one, he thought, as he stared into the canopy of trees trying to read the sky. He contemplated on the morning's events as well as the task at hand. He had to gather everything up and wait for Varick to rise, so they could get a move on. He thought about the death parade chasing that unlucky scavenger and hoped they would continue eastward and not turn around when they finished their snack. Still, it should give them enough time to clear the area as long as Varick didn't oversleep and that never happens. *But first things first. I gotta eat*, he thought as he stepped into the hidden grotto, singing to himself, "Lizzie Borden took an axe and gave her mother forty whacks. When she saw what she had done she gave her father forty-one."

*****

He sat cross-legged on the floor of the hidden grotto, looking out at the darkening landscape as he supped on some dried crackers and a few pieces of turkey jerky that were drier than the crackers. He gulped down a huge swig of water from his canteen to clear out the crumbs that were clinging to his esophagus. *Bon appétit*, he pondered while he washed down the last of his meal. It would also be the last of the jerky and crackers. He'll have to do a little work replenishing his food stores. Fortunately, wild game and fish were in abundance now if you knew where to look.

He and Varick spent too much time in this swamp recuperating. They didn't have a choice, though, because of the damage done from the inhabitants of their last stop. Damn religious zealots. They were some Old Testament, brimstone-and-fire, wrath-of-God devotees. And that priest of theirs. He was straight out of the Spanish Inquisition—*what a show.* Torquemada reincarnated with a hint of Franco. Oh well, let the dead bury the dead.

Their belongings, consisting mostly of Henry's weapon collection, were all gathered up and ready to go. The horde had moved on after the lone scavenger, clearing the way for tonight's trek, and Varick should be rising anytime now. Just as this thought appeared in his mind, a figure also appeared next him, standing tall with one hand massaging the back of his neck.

"The sleeping is rough here. I'll be more than happy to be moving on."

"Good, because our stay here is over," Henry answered, drinking more water.

"Oh. Why is that?" Varick queried while adjusting his clothing.

"Those fools attracted the wrong kind of people. I sent them stalking east, but who knows how long before they return," Henry explained as he threw his backpack over his shoulders and handed another to Varick. "Here. Yours is heavier. But you have that superhuman strength, right?" Varick grabbed the backpack and gave Henry a sideways sarcastic look.

"So where are we headed?" Henry asked.

Varick pondered the question before answering. "I have no preference. Why don't you choose?"

"Good idea," Henry said, shuddering as he thought of that last town again. The two walked out into the surrounding forest, and as soon as their silhouettes disappeared into the surrounding brush, a voice could still be heard. "By the way, don't think I forgot. You still owe me a story, man."

CHAPTER 3

The Windmill

It was dark as shit, and the two men were cautiously walking through a meadow of wild grasses reaching seven feet high. Ideal for staying out of sight or for stalking prey, Henry thought, while looking back over his shoulder again. He didn't like blind spots, and now they were treading through a blind spot the size of a small city in the middle of the night. The grass was so thick that anyone or anything could be lying in wait for them just a few feet away. But good ole Rick would let him know if there was danger lurking nearby well before it arrived. The benefits of being a bloodsucker.

Two nights had passed since they left the swamp for the open road. The first night they trekked westward along the highway, stopping at an abandoned gas station to rest at sunrise. The building was caked with dust at least an inch thick from floor to ceiling, inside and out. The dust and emptiness resembled a scene straight from one of those 1950s nuclear disaster movies where a creepy crawler gets radiated, grows fifty feet tall, and terrorizes the nearest desert town. However, there were no footprints or any other signs that the place was occupied, which was a good thing. Unfortunately, the sun beamed through the large empty windowpanes with such an intensity that Varick had to crawl inside an empty soda vending machine to sleep.

Through the windows, broken-down and abandoned cars could be seen stretched for miles up and down the highway. Beyond the highway, Henry could see the remnants of the swampland along the horizon as it blended into a landscape consisting of shrubs, bushes, and the occasional tree. The sun was high in the sky, and the breeze was light, leaving the dust unmoved. He decided that now would be a good time to forage for some more food. Ricky should be safe in here. *Unless someone thirsty comes along and wants a soda,* he thought with a grin. He reached for his backpack lying on the counter and pulled out a sling and a small hemp fiber net. After which, he grabbed his canteen and exited the building, leaving footprints in the dust.

It turned out that a few of those scattered trees were yuca, so he dug up several of the large roots and gathered a few of the leaves and flowers. There was also a stream of water that originated in the swamps and twisted its way through plain. Its surface sparkled in the sun and rippled from the movement of the numerous trout and carp swimming about underneath. He thought about catching one of them while he topped off his canteen, but he didn't feel like fish for dinner.

Henry returned later with his net filled with tubers and a couple of dead rabbits. He collected some of the dry wood and kindling lying about and constructed a makeshift fire pit behind the gas station. After skinning and cleaning the rabbits, making sure to save the blood, he wrapped a little of the meat and the flowers in the yuca leaves for supper and cut the rest into small strips for jerky. He arranged the rabbit and yuca roots strategically in the fire and sat in a canopy of shade by the back entrance.

While his dinner cooked, Henry worked on the rabbit skins, scraping them clean and oiling them before stretching them out to dry. He would add these to his collection of the various furs and skins in his backpack that he used for trade. The world had come full circle. Many of the trading practices and routes of the indigenous cultures of the Americas boomed once again. Furs, skins, and produce were being exchanged in abundance among those who were willing to trade as opposed to pillage and raid. He smiled to himself at the thought as he rummaged through the other pelts in his bag and sorted them out by color. There were patches of browns, blacks, dirty whites, and grays in assorted sizes. Some with spots and some with stripes. He studied them for a while, flipping them over in his hands, and flapping them in the air like a fan. "Or maybe I'll make myself a fur coat." He laughed.

After dinner, Henry packed their belongings, which were mostly his, and took a nap. Varick arose with the approaching evening and supped on the container of blood that Henry intentionally saved while butchering the rabbits. When Henry awoke, the two hit the road once more. They walked and talked. Well, Henry talked as he jumped from car to car, pretending the pavement was molten lava like an eight-year-old boy. A booming crash sounded with each jump, making enough noise to raise the dead. Varick watched him with an amusing grin and wondered to himself, *How is it possible that this man-child has survived this long?*

He recalled when he first met Henry, caked in dry blood, barefoot, and running for his life in the dark hours of the early morning with no one chasing him. Holding a machete. He wasn't quite wet behind the ears, but he was a nervous wreck. Now he was a hunter and a killer. Yet it was good to see that he could still enjoy himself, Varick thought with envy.

Suddenly, the booming crashes came to a stop, and the lack of noise felt harsh on the ears. Varick looked up at Henry and saw him taking a knee on the hood of a faded brown 1987 Buick Regal sedan while his left hand reached for his machete. Varick followed the direction of his gaze, and it led to a pack of feral coyotes just ten feet away, ferociously tearing away at something that oddly resembled another coyote.

Apparently, Henry's commotion and the coyote's tug-of-war over the poor animal prevented both parties from noticing each other. But now, Henry and Varick were being mad-dogged by eight pairs of bloodshot yellow eyes set above foaming mouths. One of the coyotes, a mangy-looking thing with short, dark-brown hair and half a tail, quickly jumped onto the hood of the car in front of Henry, raised his head, and gave a screeching howl. Varick's eyes squinted at the sound as six more coyotes emerged from two cars crunched together and joined the main pack. A rather large coyote with silver fur on its back and protruding fangs that dripped thick saliva stalked toward Varick. Shoulder muscles rippling beneath its fur with each step. Then it screamed like a human and fell as close to the floor as the heavy spear piercing his body would allow.

The rest of the pack responded in unison, immediately attacking both men. Vicious growls and yelps of pain, and the sound of metal clashing with bone, stirred in the air like a tornado, while blood and fur painted the abandoned cars. Varick caught one of the charging coyotes in midair and slammed his left palm into its side, turning its rib cage into mush while Henry was busy putting in work with his machete. Half of the pack had been dealt with when the mangy one appeared on top of a rusty RV and howled again. There was a brief silence that was broken by the sound of a hundred running paws and angry barks approaching fast from the highway ahead. Henry and Varick looked at each other, deciding what to do next. Henry pulled his spear from the silver-back's body, and then they jumped from car to car and over the highway railing into darkness with coyotes in chase.

*****

They ran along a cement embankment below the highway for close to an hour before they lost the coyotes, who seemed to break the chase at a certain distance from their howling leader as if ordered to do so like obedient soldiers. Exhaustion was taking its toll on Henry, and sunlight could be seen making its way above the horizon, which meant that Varick had to find a place where the sun didn't shine, and quick.

It was decided that they should hide out under an overpass for the day and recuperate. Varick wedged himself under the off-ramp, and Henry covered his body with branches and leaves to conceal him from the sun and lookie-loos. Henry thought about getting some shut-eye too but couldn't get those coyotes off his mind, so he sat and waited. He woke up with a stiff neck and goose bumps covering his skin from the chill in the air. The sun was low in the sky, and Varick was still resting. He checked the time on his silver pocket watch. Almost 5:00 p.m.

"Where did you pick that little item up?"

Henry jerked in surprise at the comment. "I got it from one of those scavengers the other day. He was dying for me to have it." He laughed at his own joke as he rose from his sitting position.

"You ready to move?" he asked Varick.

"Yes, but maybe we should stay off the highway," suggested Varick.

And now on the third night they were walking in the middle of an overgrown savannah, practically blind, and with no sign of shelter from the inevitable sun once again.

Although for the moment it was Henry all by himself surrounded by tall grasses rustling in the light breeze with no idea of what lay ahead, behind, or to the flank. Varick, determined to find shelter, darted ahead with lighting speed to recon the area. Henry's eyes started to twitch and blink uncontrollably. It was a nervous condition he had since he was a boy. Anyone who knew him well enough could tell when he was stressed out or ready to explode. "Come on. Where are you?"

Varick landed softly next to Henry, right on cue. "What is it you say now and then? Don't get your *chones* in a bunch."

"Shit, man, why do you always do that? Did you find anything?" Henry asked

"Yes. There are some structures about two miles out where the meadow ends. They appeared to be abandoned."

"Well, let's go. Before the sun rises and gives you a deadly tan," Henry quipped.

As they neared their destination, they treaded lightly and stopped under a tree with branches that practically touched the ground. Hidden beneath the leafy awning, they observed what seemed to be another forgotten town for movement and signs of habitation. The latter would be difficult to spot as most people preferred to keep their existence a secret.

All the structures held their shape but had been consumed by the forest, giving the town an appearance of an emerald city twinkling in the moonlight. Henry thought he saw what looked like a windmill poking out from under some tangled vines, but he thought it was much too small.

"This isn't a town," he said as he walked out from under the large tree.

"Are you certain?" asked Varick.

"Yeah. You see that?" he answered and nodded his head toward the windmill. "This is a put-put course. You know, minigolf. Come on."

Enough time had passed for the moon to inch closer to the horizon while they searched the perimeter, hacking away at the jungle before they found a possible entrance. Henry's machete struck contact with metal underneath the foliage. The iron gate fell off its rusty hinges when they pulled out the entangled vines that were supporting it, exposing the waist-high thickets of grass and bush that lay on the other side.

They entered the park area keeping low and keeping quiet, with Varick using his nocturnal bat vision to lead the way. Henry could only see as far as his outstretched hand, and after that it was pitch-black. It was darker in the park than it was in the meadow, Henry was thinking, when Varick gave the signal to halt. He crept up next to Varick and waited quietly while Varick observed and listened.

"There was movement," Varick whispered.

"Could have been an animal," Henry said.

"I thought I heard breathing. Small human breathing," Varick responded.

Henry gave Varick a confused look. "So what do we do?" Varick continued to observe the area without answering, and then he started forward again. They made their way to the biggest structure in the park, with the assumption that it was the old customer-service station, with hopes of finding an old map or brochure of the place.

Varick lifted Henry with ease to a small window in the rear of the building that could be seen under the overgrowth. Henry was prepared to break the glass when he noticed that the window was ajar because of some thick vines that had wedged themselves between the window and the latch. He pulled out a knife and cut away at the vines, until the window was clear and pushed it open to the complaint of the flaking layers of rust. Then he squeezed himself through the opening and landed hands and headfirst on a dust and rat-crap coated floor with a crunch. "Shit!" He pushed himself up, smashing more crap with the palms of his hands and called for Varick, who was already standing next to him, smirking.

"Damnit!" Henry exclaimed while he wiped his hands on his pants. The sound of his voice bounced off the walls with an echo, and they discovered that they were standing in a bathroom. Henry tested the faucets for water, but the pipes merely groaned like old ogres and sputtered out dust. The inside of the building was a wide-open space lined with display cabinets containing leftover golf accessories and a service kiosk in the center. The second floor consisted of broken video games and shelves of forgotten prizes, stuffed animals wearing coats of dust like a second fur. They searched the building for anything useful, but it was obvious that the place had been abandoned and rummaged through several times over before the forest reclaimed all. Like everywhere else.

Henry pulled out his watch and announced that it was approaching 5:00 a.m. Both he and Varick searched for an opening in the foliage to view the sky and noticed they couldn't find one. The outer jungle covered the building with such an intensity that it prevented the rays of the sun and the moon from making their way through the building. It also kept the temperature inside cool and crisp. Henry dropped his bag and sighed in relief as he stretched his arms above his head. Varick lowered the bag he was carrying to the ground and walked about the area peering into the dark spaces, looking for trouble, or maybe food.

"This could be a good spot to hide out—not that we're hiding from anything," Henry said as he massaged his lower back. "There's plenty of space, and it's nice and dark just how you like it."

"Yes. Our luck seems to have changed," Varick stated with skepticism as he continued to scan the area.

"Don't worry, man. I'll have a look around in the morning. You know, to make sure we're not intruding," Henry said in response to Varick's skepticism. "Besides, I need to find some more water.

Once they settled in, Henry relaxed with an early breakfast of rabbit jerky and yuca. Afterward, he cleaned his weapons and took inventory of their supplies. Varick chose to rest in an office space in the far corner of the lower floor where he discovered and old sofa. The sun was moving above the horizon in the east, but the night was permanent inside customer service.

*****

"Are you certain there were only two?" asked an old voice worn from years of tobacco use and whiskey drinking.

"Two is all I saw. The east gate is broken too," answered a young girl with dirt on her cheeks and a bruise under her right eye.

"Hmm" was all that the old voice offered while gray, squinted, and jaundiced eyes stared down the little girl from over a round bumpy nose pockmarked with black pores. The little girl looked down in shame and terror without uttering a word. *If I don't say nuthin' I might get a backhand, but if I say something and he don't like it, then I will get the lash for sure*, she thought. There was a group of boys and girls huddled at the foot of the throne who were obviously thinking the same thing judging, from the pleading looks on their faces. *Please don't make him mad,* the look said.

The man with the old voice leaned forward in his "throne" and placed his elbows on his knees. The wooden makeshift throne creaked in the background as he gave the crowd of young innocents the once-over with a look that implied guilty.

"I wonder how they could have stumbled upon our home?" the man asked no one in particular. "Is it pure luck? Or did a little bird show them the way? I wonder?" This last statement was directed toward the waif with the black eye standing in the middle of the dank room. He stared her down for what seemed like forever until he finally said, "We'll have to wait and see what there up to, I guess." He gave a sigh of boredom like a king who has grown tired of his court jesters.

"I'm hungry! Where is my breakfast!" he yelled and leaned back in his throne. He brushed back his shaggy salt-and-pepper hair—

mostly salt—with his hand exposing a receding hairline that gave his forehead a widow's peak Bela Lugosi would be envious of. At the abrupt announcement, the girl turned in a flash and ran down a long concrete hallway until she faded into the black, leaving behind the echo of hurried footsteps.

Dreadful thoughts raced through her mind as she entered a boiler room with various-sized pots and pans, and other cooking utensils hanging from the overhead pipes. "Why was he looking at me? Did I do something wrong? Is he going to send me to the pit?" The room was lined with shelves that appeared to be taken from a cafeteria kitchen stacked with assorted cooking and dishware. There was an olive-skinned preadolescent girl stirring the contents of a soup pot on a wood-burning stove, giving orders to a boy of about six years. Both were wearing grease-spotted aprons. The boy's apron was a bit too big for him, and it dragged on the floor in front of his feet, causing him to trip every now and then.

"Hurry up! He's hungry!" she yelled at the two kitchen workers, panting and catching her breath.

"It almost done!" the juvenile cook yelled back while she observed the thick stew she was stirring. Her hanging hair blocked her face as she spoke, and the rising steam from the pot embraced the strands like a misty octopus.

"Get me a plate," she snapped at her assistant. He shuffled as quickly as his oversized apron would allow him to move without accident and moseyed over to one of the shelves along the walls and reached up and grabbed a white plate from the top of a tall stack of dishes. When the boy removed the plate, the stack teetered toward the brink of collapse but held steady like the Tower of Pisa. He delivered the plate to his chef and went back to his business of busy work.

"I could hear him yelling all the way back hear. What happened?" the cook asked.

"He's always yelling," the bruised girl said in a melancholic tone.

"Yeah, but he sounds really mad this time," the cook said while grabbing a piece of corn bread from a cast-iron pan and placing it on the plate.

"Somebody's up top. In the gardens."

The cook froze with ladle and plate in hand and looked up at the bruised girl with dark eyes round as macadamias. "You mean people? Live ones?"

"Yes."

The cook handed the plate, along with a spoon and cup of coffee to the girl, and glanced at the bruise under her eye. "Did he do that to you, Gina?" The girl looked away, took the plate and cup from the cook, and turned to leave.

"How many are there?" the dark-eyed cook asked.

"I don't know. I only saw two," Gina answered back as she rushed out into the hallway.

"What? You saw 'em?" the cook yelled after her, but there was no answer.

The throne room was empty when she returned except for two boys who were setting up a table complete with tablecloth in front of their lounging would-be king. He looked at her with suspicion as she approached with his breakfast. *This one needs to be watched,* he thought. *She's resourceful.* Gina placed the plate and drink on the table and stepped back. Standing at attention, she watched him while he devoured the stew and gulped the coffee down without breathing. He set the cup on the table and belched with a nefarious giggle. After slurping up the last of his stew with the corn bread, the two attendees gathered the dishes and table and left the room.

He wiped his mouth with the sleeve of his beige corduroy coat, rested in his chair, and gazed up at the cement ceiling to collect his thoughts. "First you will round up Frederick and Timothy and repair the east gate before any of the dead ones get a chance to roam in here. Then you will go and see what these intruders' intentions are." He explained this smoothly to Gina without looking down at her. Before she could answer he summoned her with the snap of his fingers. She approached him, and he grabbed her by the hair and pulled her close. "And remember to keep out of sight," he whispered in her face. She could smell his breakfast on his breath and see its remnants in between his yellow teeth as he spoke. He leered at her and raised his free hand to her face with a clenched fist. *Don't cry,* she told herself. *Just take it.* His leer quickly changed to a smile, yellow teeth and all.

He opened his fist and ran his index finger down her face and tapped the tip of her nose with a boop.

Then he shoved her to the ground and pulled a pipe from the breast pocket of his coat. "Now, go and do as you were told," he told her before lighting his pipe and disappearing behind a cloud of smoke.

*****

After cleaning his weapons and finishing the last of the yuca root, Henry sat in the dark on a tablecloth he scrounged from a supply closet, bored. "Hey!" he yelled out and listened to his voice echo in the large space. He was too restless to take a morning nap, so he chose to explore the grounds of their new location.

He hid their belongings under the service counter and covered them with the tablecloth. He thought about exiting through the front doors but then opted for the bathroom window in case anyone was watching the place. After concealing the window with leaves and branches, he walked out into the forest and headed straight toward the windmill with water on his mind. He figured it would be a good place to start his search. As he made his way into the bush, he noticed that the closer he got to the windmill, the vegetation receded more into somewhat managed growth. It went from waist high to knee high, and there were trees spread out in different areas of the golf park, with vines creeping around their trunks but not covering the limbs and leaves.

When he arrived at the windmill, he took a seat on a moss- and fern-covered wooden fence and pulled out a piece of rabbit jerky from his shirt pocket. While working his jaw muscles on the jerky and zoning out on the thicket-covered ground in front of him, small pockets of greenish-yellow orbs began to poke themselves through the leaves. Henry blinked several times and stuck his neck out like an ostrich to get a closer look. "Is that squash?" the question slipped from his lips unconsciously as he *stood* up and walked to the orbs. He knelt and shuffled the leaves around and found a group of green squash growing under the thicket. He looked around and then picked the largest squash and put it in his hemp net, thinking about how he would prepare it later.

His fortune didn't end there. As he moved from hole to hole, there was a patch of vegetables at each location. He found beans at the alligator, and there were onions at the pirate ship, carrots at the Paul Bunyan hole, and beets at the old lady's shoe—"*who had so many children she didn't know what to do.*" He made sure to only take what he was going to use and left the rest untouched.

On his way back to the customer-service building with a net full of fresh produce, he took notice of the sporadic trees with the vine-covered trunks and thought it curious how the vines did not engulf the entire tree like everywhere else. He approached one of the trees in his path and saw that the vines wrapping around its trunk were grapes in midseason. He hadn't seen grapes on the vine since he was a boy in Central California. The aroma of dirt and tortillas seared his senses. Looking up into the trees' shelter, he saw that there were avocados ripening high above on the farthest branches. Apparently, someone had already pruned the low-hanging fruits.

The other trees were citrus of all sorts: lemons, limes, oranges, grapefruit, and tangerines. Each one cleverly disguised with overgrowth and vines and made to appear barren. There were many other trees way off in the distance that may have been apple or peach as well. This was someone's, or had been someone's, private orchard, Henry pondered. Where did everyone go? The thought sent chills up his spine and suddenly he felt like he was being watched. He may not have the senses of a vampire, but he knew when he was being watched.

When he returned to the customer-service building Varick was up and about pacing the floor in the main area with his hands clasped behind his back like a general.

"Good evening," Henry greeted him and dropped his net on the service counter. "There's a lot of stuff growing out there. Only problem is it's too well managed to be the work of Mother Nature."

Varick glanced at Henry's net and continued to pace. "I need to find food" was all he offered before leaving the building, departing through the window as well.

"Sometimes he can be so rude," Henry quipped and then took a carrot from his net and chomped it down like a cartoon bunny with a bit of rabbit jerky while he laughed at the irony.

*****

Six hungry eyes peeked out from an ivy-covered ventilation duct near one of the courses' structures shaped like a hippo and watched the man with the machete as he picked vegetables and stuffed them in his net. They thought it funny that he didn't take everything but only one or two items from each patch. *Most people would take it all and burn down the buildings right before they tortured and had their way with us*, Gina thought. *Or at least that's what the Dean tells us, which is why it's so important to keep the gardens a secret.*

"What should we do?" whispered Timothy, anxious to act.

"Just watch for now," Gina whispered back.

"But they're taking stuff. The Dean is gonna kill us if we don't stop him." Frederick was only five years old, but he was big for his age. He was squatting next to Timothy, holding a small axe in his trembling hands. Unfortunately, his courage didn't match his size.

"We don't know if there are more yet. So just wait."

Frederick let out a small sigh of relief at Gina's instructions and hoped that Timmy didn't notice. Timmy was always teasing him and calling him chicken. He also hoped that Timmy didn't notice how much the axe was shaking in his hands. He didn't think he could kill anyone. Even if it meant being sent to the pit.

"How long are we gonna wait?" Timothy asked with a hint of impatience.

Timothy, or Timmy, wanted to kill someone or something and quick. He was eager to prove himself too… And it wasn't often that the gardens had intruders. He was honored to have been chosen to spy on these strangers who would come here to take and destroy everything he works for. For an eleven-year-old, he was bold, and the one thing he wanted the most was to take Gina's place as the Dean's number one.

"Keep quiet!" Gina snapped at him, and the trio continued to watch in silence.

When the man's net was half-full, he walked toward some of the trees and picked the fruit he could reach without climbing. The children stalked him throughout the park until he reached the customer-service building and entered through a back window.

"Now what?" Timmy was looking at the building with the angry and pouting expression of a spoiled brat about to throw a tantrum.

"We'll watch and wait for as long as it takes," Gina said calmly.

"But he stole from us. We need to get him and whoever else is with him!" Timmy pleaded resentfully.

"It's not our decision," Gina said. "Besides, you really think you can take 'em? You and Frederick? The saviors of the garden." She grinned with satisfaction at the insult.

Timothy grunted in disgust at her comment and punched Frederick in the arm, who was giggling behind his hand. "She's making fun of you too, dummy," Timothy scolded, and Frederick stopped giggling and stared down at his feet in embarrassment. He was less embarrassed with the comment than with the reality that he was too chicken to stand up to Timmy. Timmy was right about him, and they both knew it.

Their shadows disappeared, and their stomachs grumbled in unison while they watched from inside the old shoe. "This is taking forever," Timothy groaned. "We already missed dinner. I'm gonna go and get some apples," he said as he stood to leave.

Gina grabbed his arm and yanked him back to the ground with ease, and Timothy gave her a surprised look. "Shut up, stupid," she growled while she focused on the small rear window.

"What is it?" Frederick asked while Timothy rubbed his arm, grimacing in pain.

"Someone's coming out," Gina answered, pointing her chin toward the window.

The foliage covering the window was moving aside, and a slender figure slithered out the window and down the wall like a reptile. When the figure reached the ground, it walked a few paces on its hands and flipped over onto its feet with the ease of a gymnast. Timothy and Frederick looked at each other in disbelief while Gina kept her focus on the slender figure. She watched as its shadow transformed into shapes resembling Rorschach blotches blending in with the shadows of the night as it crept its way along.

"Did you see that?" Timmy and Frederick blurted out simultaneously from over Gina's shoulders.

Just as she was about to explain that she was as bewildered as they were, the figure stopped in midstep as it writhed into the brush and turned its head in the direction of the three spies. For a moment, Gina was sure that the figure could see her spying from within the old shoe. She ducked, placing her back against the interior of the shoe wall, and squeezed her eyes shut. She could feel her pulse beating in her temples. When she opened her eyes, Frederick and Timothy were squatting in front of her in shock and wondering what in the hell they should do.

"I think it saw us," she said.

"What?" Frederick cried and then quickly put his hand over his mouth.

She stood slowly, moving as if silence mattered now, and peeked out the shoelace eyehole. It was gone. Perhaps. It was too dark to tell.

"It's time to go back."

"What about the one in there?" Timothy asked, pointing his rusty buck knife toward the customer-service building. "And that other thing?"

Gina stared nervously through the shoelace eyehole into the shadows of the forest, trying to spot the figure. She would feel a lot better if she knew where it was before they moved. "Let's go," she said as she turned toward the boys. "We have to report this to the Dean. He'll know what to do." She really did hope that he would know what to do. In spite of all of the cruelties suffered at his hands, and the ominous threat of the pit, he did keep them safe. He raised all of them, and protected them, until it was time to go beyond the quarry and begin the journey they were preparing for. This last thought gave her a sense of encouragement, and she urged the other two on as they headed back to their home.

*****

"Mmm. So juicy," Henry exclaimed out loud as he relished the tree-ripened flavor of one of the apples he picked earlier. He was sitting on the counter of the reception area with his legs hanging over the edge. *I can't wait to taste those fuzzy peaches*, he thought as he swiped his mouth with the palm of his hand. *The only thing I need now is a television and a couch.* He reminisced a little about when he used to kick back on the living room couch after attending a partial day of school: well-baked, red-eyed, remote control resting on his chest and cartoons on the screen. He smiled and took a drink from his canteen. "A beer would be nice too." Movement reflected off the glass of one of the display cabinets. "Welcome back. That was fast?"

Varick ignored the comment and peered around at the spotlights glowing in the display cases illuminating the dust-laden goods and prizes. After which, he gave Henry an impatient, questioning look.

"What? They popped on by themselves about twenty minutes ago. Probably on a timer or something," Henry said, shrugging his shoulders. "But nothing else works. I checked."

"Interesting. Where is the power source?" Varick turned gracefully, appearing to survey the landscape through the building walls. "It cannot have withstood the elements of nature unattended," he thought aloud. "That explains the goats."

"Goats?" Henry stated while dabbing fruit juice from around his mouth with a thin rag.

"Yes. Where I fed this evening. It wasn't far off. There was a group of goats sleeping amongst some fallen trees and briar bushes that were obviously situated to keep them penned in."

Henry nodded as if in agreement. "Yeah. I found a shitload of gardens out there hidden under a bunch of weeds and stuff. There was an orchard too. That's where I found all this produce." He gestured with his chin toward his hemp net. "Somebody's definitely been putting in a lot of work here. I think we should leave before we meet up with the gardeners," he suggested. "Remember the last town?"

"They know we're here," Varick said.

"What?"

He gave Henry a—"you should know better by now" look and explained about the children in the shoe. "They were afraid but not of us."

"Maybe the dead ones?"

Varick concentrated for a moment. "Perhaps."

Henry remembered the eerie feeling of being spied on when he was gathering food. "If it's too good to be true, then it is." He sighed as a fruit-filled cornucopia passed in his mind melded with an image of himself seated at a royal feast with bunches of grapes in one hand and a chalice of wine in the other. Shades of purple stained his cheeks and the ruffled collars of his silk shirt. "That settles it. We're leaving."

"I agree. We should depart," Varick said, observing the area. "However, there's not much left of the night, so we'll have to depart at dusk. Unless you're willing to carry me."

Henry gave him a narrow, side-eyed expression accompanied with a "tsk!" "That's alright, man. Are you sure though? We could leave now."

"I'm quite sure. Besides, there's no guarantee of finding shelter before sunrise. And I am not going to hide under a bridge again like some troll." Varick's face tightened when he said this.

"I guess we could kick it here until tomorrow evening. We're just gonna have to keep *truchas*. Maybe tell a story to pass the time," Henry said this while scanning the interior of the building and making sure to make eye contact with Varick at the last statement. His sharp features offered no response. "Come on. Tell me about Lizzie Borden, man. We got time to kill." He stuck out his bottom lip in a pouty expression and sank to one knee with hands folded in prayer. "Pleeease."

*****

Timothy pushed the metal service door and held it open for Gina and Frederick as they stepped over the high threshold into the short cement hallway with an industrial-sized circuit-breaker box attached to the wall on the right. After he closed the door behind them and slid the iron security bar into place, he studied the square door for a second wondering, again, about the faded, chipped red-and-yellow paint markings. He couldn't figure out letters like Gina. Just another reason why he hated her. The Dean's little pet. Even though she tried to teach him, he still couldn't get it. Damn her! "Letters are stupid anyways," he grumbled before turning to catch up with the others.

The three walked to the end of the hallway and turned left into a larger corridor lined with an intricate network of pipes and cables. Gina led the way, turning a corner every now and then. They were moving through an underground tunnel system that served as a highway that sprawled out from the generator room in the center, with each tunnel leading to a golf-course attraction or utility structure. The dimly lit halls were dank like a dungeon, and the lights flickered on and off in some areas. The entire golf course was powered by one generator, which meant that certain portions of the park were given limited energy, or none at all.

The generator was fueled with bioenergy sources and maintained by the children. But it was the Dean who converted the generator and taught them how to create biofuel from the algae collected from the moat surrounding the castle and the various ponds throughout the golf course.

Their empty stomachs reminded them that they missed dinner, and Timothy started to complain again. Their pace quickened driven by their hunger and the fear of the Dean's impatience. Yet there was a hint of eagerness in all of them as each one was determined to report the findings of their mission in hopes of gaining favor with their leader. They ran around like rats in a maze until they hit a hallway at the far end of the golf course that led to the castle. The Dean's private residence.

CHAPTER 4

A Bit of History

Henry lay on the floor in a comfortable pile of tablecloths gathered from the storage closet, using one of the backpacks as a pillow, with his arms folded behind his head. He had one leg folded over the other, with his foot subconsciously swaying back and forth as he peered out a large window, trying to find a crack in the forest covering the building so he could view the night sky. He could dimly hear the soft footsteps of Varick's pacing in the background of his foggy concentration.

"Well. Tell me. What do you know about the Bordens and Fall River?" Varick questioned Henry as he strode past his prone body with hands clasped behind his back the way he often does. Looking like the inspector general. He eyed Henry as he passed him waiting for an answer.

"Huh? Oh, nothing really. Just that she murdered her parents with an axe when they were sleeping. And that she did it for the money. You know the inheritance because they were rich," Henry replied in a relaxed tone. "Pretty much what I know from the song."

"You're quite correct. You know nothing about the Fall River killings. First of all, the limerick is pure propaganda created as a distraction to ease the tensions in the area and to relieve the suspicions that had been brought to light as a result of the Borden murders." Varick stopped in his tracks at the end of this statement and stared in thought at some dusty T-shirts in a display cabinet. When Henry noticed what he was staring at, he reminded himself to grab one of those T-shirts before they left the minigolf course. *It'll make a great souvenir*, he thought.

Henry's only response to Varick's statement was a mumble. He knew by Varick's behavior that interrupting him wasn't a good idea. There were times when he couldn't get a word out of him for all the blood in the world, but when he travelled back to his days of yore, there was no cutting him off. The best thing to do was to sit and listen. *Next time I'll watch what I wish for* flashed in his mind like a neon warning sign. Varick's dark eyes seemed to glow on his sullen face as he recounted the details of his extended life. Henry didn't know if it was some sort of vampire hypnosis trick, but whenever he shared an experience from his past, Henry swore he could see and smell aromas, pleasant and putrid, rising around Varick when he spoke and heard melodies seeping from his ears as if they were emanating from an orchestra pit.

Henry sat up and pulled out a peach from his net as Varick continued to pace until he finally took a spot on the floor in front of Henry sitting crossed-legged.

He glanced at the peach with curiosity, adjusted his form, and straightened his leather coat before proceeding with his much-anticipated tale.

*****

The hallway leading to the Dean's abode was unlike all the other corridors with their cold gray walls extending into oblivion. Caution signs, noisy pipes, and the hum of electrical cables were nonexistent here. And the lighting never faltered. As they neared the service door, the smell of old leather, dust, and pipe tobacco began to rise above the odor of mold and cold cement. The scent seeped from around the door frame and floated in front of the door in an imagined fog surrounding a painting of an owl perched above a basket of fruit in the middle of a pair of curved, pointed staffs. Gina remembered overhearing the Dean calling them elephant tusks. He had some older kids who weren't here anymore paint the image a few years ago. Then he explained to us one day that it was some sort of symbol representing greatness and that it belonged to his family, of which he was the lone survivor. He called it a coat of arms.

Gina reached out to pry open the door, when Frederick grabbed her by the wrist and looked up. Gina's eyes followed his to the hanging wooden board with a fist and a door carved onto it. On the right side of this was a number 1 carved in the same manner. "Knock first."

"Thanks," she said with a sigh of relief and gave Frederick a grateful look. Her excitement and trepidation had her forgetting about the rules, which should never happen if you want to keep the Dean happy.

"Enter, please." They could hear the distant and muffled response coming from the other side of the door. Gina and Timothy pushed the heavy door together and hopped over the threshold. Frederick didn't move. They looked back at him as if they were about to say, "What's the holdup?" when he cautiously stepped into the large room. It was lit by several standing lamps in each corner of the room, as well as beeswax candles placed here and there. The Dean with his back to them, and arms folded, was staring at a large map that covered most of the wall he was facing like a tapestry. The dark-brown suede patches on the elbows of his tan corduroy coat were worn thin.

They walked around a pair of cracked, brown leather chairs and stood huddled in silence in front of an antique wooden desk with a smoldering pipe and marble ashtray sitting next to assorted statues and open books. The Dean commented out loud about the topography of the Middle Ages before turning toward the young trio. He scrutinized them with his cold gray eyes as he pulled his wooden desk chair closer to him and plopped down onto the padded leather seat. "Report," he said while lighting his pipe with a candle. It was more of a demand than a question, thought Gina.

Their anticipation had turned to anxiety when it came time to speak, and they stood there speechless, huddled in silence.

"Well?" he asked in a low voice as thick smoke exited the nostrils of his bulbous bulging nose, hiding the lower half of his face.

Only his eyes could be seen above the cloudy curtain, allowing him to glare at them with impatience.

They looked at one another in confusion and debated who should go first. All speaking at once in a cacophony of chatter. "Tell him. You're his favorite," Timothy said, nodding toward Gina.

"Bsut we all saw it," she snapped back.

"I don't wanna tell him," Frederick whimpered while shaking his head left to right.

"Sissy," Timothy said, raising a hand at him. "Leave him alone. You're always picking on him."

"Enough!"

They quickly snapped their jaws shut and jumped to attention, realizing where they were and stood side by side facing the Dean.

"The girl will speak."

Timothy and Frederick quickly looked down at the ground in submission as Gina stepped closer to the wooden desk and nodded her head in respect before speaking. "There's only two of them. The same ones I saw earlier. We didn't see anybody else." She paused before continuing and looked over her shoulder at her companions, who were still facing the ground. The Dean was refilling his pipe with tobacco and hadn't noticed her hesitation. Thank goodness. "One of them raided the fruit orchards and stole vegetables."

"Of course. They'll eat everything and move on. Like locusts," he spoke as if they weren't present and ranted on about how no one wants to help bake the bread while Gina was bursting at the seams to tell him about what else they saw. She remembered how the dark shape twisted as fast as dust and leaves in a whirlpool to look at her when they were hiding in the shoe. And she was pretty sure that it smelled her too.

"Did you fix the gate like I told you?"

"Yes," Timothy and Frederick answered in unison, begging for the Dean's attention.

"Good. Before you know it, those abominations will overrun us if we're not vigilant." He tapped his pipe on the edge of the ashtray to empty the ashes and set it down next to a small clay figurine with no head and a protruding stomach and oversized breasts. "What of the other. You did say there was two?"

Gina swallowed to clear the nervous lump in her throat before speaking. "The other one..." She looked back at the two boys again.

"Do you need their permission to speak, girl? Out with it."

"The other one didn't leave the building until nighttime, and we don't know where he went." The Dean raised a furry, gray eyebrow and gave her a stern look. *He's getting angry*, she thought. "He was too fast to follow. He..."

The two boys noticed her hesitation and quickly came to her rescue. "It walked on its hands like they were feet!" Timothy blurted.

"It climbed the walls too. We saw it! And then it disappeared," said Frederick.

"Yeah. It went invisible," Timothy added.

The Dean looked at the boys and then back at Gina in frustration. She shrugged her shoulders nervously. "He climbed out the bathroom window and disappeared," she struggled to explain while nodding her head from side to side, searching for more to say.

"Yeah, and tell him how he moved like a snake!" Frederick whined.

They were scared and hungry, he thought. They wouldn't dare lie to him. They're well aware of the consequences. Nevertheless, his interest was sparked, and he was growing weary. "What is this nonsense? Have you gone mad?" he said, surprisingly calm. The three glanced at each other and stood still, waiting for the real tongue-lashing when he asked, "It must be your hunger? Go. There's food for you in the kitchen. Tell Ruth that you've been approved for seconds."

Three big salivating smiles turned and ran to the door, but as they were exiting the large room, he called out to Gina. "Stay. I will have a word with you." The boys looked at her with fear and sympathy.

"Oh no," Frederick whispered. "Don't worry. Go and eat," Gina said to them with that reassuring look that always made them feel safe, even Timothy, and they ran fast to fill their bellies.

*****

As Varick's velvet voice painted the tale on canvas, Henry found himself standing on a crowded walkway of a puddled, cobblestoned street breathing in burning coal and musty river water. Heavy chatter and clopping horse hooves clashed with wooden carriage wheels and young boys yelling. "Extra, extra. News flash!" Prim-and-proper women wearing bonnets, some carrying prayer books or grocery baskets, while others covered the lower half of their faces with silk handkerchiefs and a sprig of lavender to avoid the stench of the hidden alleyways they frequented to purchase their much-needed laudanum. Rising above all the commotion, a steam whistle blared loud enough to part the clouds, announcing the end of another overworked day for the newly emerging class of the underpaid wage worker.

The industrial revolution was in full swing, and ingenuity, ambition, and American know-how were leading the way into the twentieth century with advances in manufacturing and commerce. The Fall River skyline was colored with oaks, pines, and church steeples. Smokestacks exhaled black clouds in the shape of dollar signs for the families that held control of the Quequechan River and the region's coal industry. Underneath this skyline, recently arrived immigrants trying to climb that hill existed side by side with the native-born descendants of WASP immigrants who resided on the top of that hill, metaphorically and figuratively, in the case of Fall River.

Henry listened intently as the words flowed from Varick's mouth like a cool stream. He hung on to every verb and noun and forgot all about the peach in his hand as Varick provided a description of a Victorian-era community in the throes of societal change and progress. Temperate women, young and old, uniting en masse to fight for the right to vote and a sober nation. African Americans climbing their way up the social ladder and continuing to deal with the realities of post-Reconstruction in a state that was home to the Radical Republicans, the Abolitionist Movement, and the 54th. The first African American regiment in the United States.

The docks were busy with thick-armed stevedores soaked with sweat in fifty-degree weather, well-dressed merchants in top hats giving orders with their brass canes, and grimy derelicts slyly keeping watch for the choicest pockets to pick. There were immaculate churchgoers singing psalms and greeting the newly arrived wide-eyed immigrants as they exited the crowded ships in an endless stream, resembling ants in a colony only to be confronted by native-born descendants of European settlers protesting the invasion of their nation. Native-born locals who proudly boasted of their blue-blooded ancestry stemming from the *Mayflower's* intrusion on the Mashpee civilization screamed in outrage at the foreign families and groups of single men walking down the ship planks. Meanwhile, two bloodshot-eyed Mashpee were sitting on a pile of rope dressed like Victorian gentlemen in third-hand clothing, sharing a bottle of fire water and watching the scene in confusion.

*****

Henry was wiping peach juice from the end of his elbow. The juice had streamed down the length of his forearm from the forgotten peach as he sat in captivation. "Wow! You know what, man? It sounds more like the sixties not the eighteen whatevers. There's Bible thumpers, boycotts, and White people bitching about *braceros*." He took a huge bite from the peach. "Mmm."

Varick frowned at the last phrase. "People from Mexico who came to the US to work back in the day," Henry explained. "It was some kind of government program. My *tia* told me about it when I was little."

Varick nodded in comprehension. "Times change. Humans don't" was all that he offered.

"Hmm?" Henry quipped while gnawing on the pit of the peach, sucking out pulp from the nooks and crannies of the large seed. "I was about to ask how you know all of this, but your old ass has been everywhere and every time." He tossed the pit over his shoulder, and it landed behind the reception counter with a thunk. Then he wiped his hands on the thighs of his pants and relaxed on an elbow, Greek style, again ready to hear some more.

Varick smirked at the reality of Henry's comment and attitude. "Yes. I spent some time on the Eastern Seaboard in the eighteen nineties on my way to the Pacific. Coincidentally, I had arrived in the

States just after Ms. Borden and her retinue had returned from a trip to Europe, where many believe the secrets that spurred the legend of Lizzie Borden sprang to life.

*****

The Dean relaxed in his seat and gestured in the direction of the cracked leather chairs in front of the desk as a sign for Gina to take a sit down. "Sit. You've been working hard. Your body must be tired."

She took a step toward the chairs and hesitated. This could be one of his tricks. He loves to play tricks, she thought. He watched her nervous behavior, and a thin hint of a smile touched his lips. "Go ahead." He gestured again, and she stepped in front of one of the chairs and gently lowered herself as if she were about to lay on a bed of nails.

The Dean leaned forward and set his elbows on the desk, clasped his hands, and touched his fingertips to his mouth in contemplation. Gina sat with her hands placed on the arms of the leather chair, while he studied her with furrowed black and white eyebrows as thick as caterpillars. "Those two can be so tiresome at times." He glanced at the door and back at Gina. "Weak minds. They lack the mental fortitude to be reliable leaders. Especially Timothy. Though he believes he's the strongest."

He continued to speak, never losing eye contact with Gina as she sat motionless in the oversized chair. "They're not like you. None of them are. Are they?" The question wasn't meant for her, and she knew better not to answer. He rose from his seat, removed his beige corduroy coat, and draped it over the back of the chair. "So why don't you explain to me what you really observed," he said as he walked around the desk until he passed her. She could feel his presence behind her and could picture him with his arms folded standing over her like a viper waiting to strike.

Just tell him what you saw. Don't be scared. "Well, we watched for a long time like you said to, and the first one came out while the sun was still up and raided the—"

"Yes, yes," he cut her off. "He stole some fruit. Tell me about the other one?" The sound of his voice faded at the end of his statement as if he was turning away from her.

The leather under her squeaked as she sat up in the big chair and straightened her posture before speaking again. She also remembered the bruise on her cheek. "The other one didn't come out till it got dark. He was way sneakier than the other one. And we wouldn't have saw him but..."

The Dean, who was examining a large bookshelf, turned to look at her when she paused. "But?" he asked while observing her expression.

"I think he wanted us to see him. Like he knew we were watching. And the way he moved. It was like a snake, but more like its shadow. Or a mist," she whispered with a blank stare as if hypnotized. She hadn't planned on making this last statement, but she could feel it being whispered in her ear, and she repeated it. "Mist," she whispered.

She had The Dean's full attention, and he was facing her with a look of doubt combined with moderate anticipation. "You said this one did not exit the building until the sun went down?"

It took her a moment to respond because the question was being enveloped by the whisper. She shook her head and struggled to speak. Her tongue felt swollen. "Yes."

He turned to face the bookshelf again and continued to examine it. "Interesting. Would you be able to describe him?" he asked as he grabbed a book from the third shelf and pulled it out halfway before pushing it back in place.

She jumped in her seat as an image of the thing that turned and looked at her when she was in the shoe flickered in her mind like a broken lightbulb. "Dark eyes," she said. "It had dark eyes and black hair. The skin glowed like...like the 'dead ones,' just not so pale. And he wasn't dirty. The other one he was like all the others, but this one he was cleaner somehow. I can't explain it."

"Is there anything else?" The Dean asked without emotion.

"No," she said and then broke off in thought. "Wait. There is something."

"Yes?" the Dean asked, trying not to appear anxious.

"I think he could smell us," she said.

The Dean raised an eyebrow. "Smell?"

"Yeah. I think it was sniffing us." She looked down at her feet in embarrassment when she said this. "I don't know. It just seemed like he knew where we were before he saw us."

"Hmm." Followed by a long silence was all there was. Gina sat, still waiting for anything, something, to happen. He stepped in front of her, saying nothing, only observing and then: "My apologies for keeping you so long. You must be ravenous by now." He reached out his hand to help her out of her seat. She looked at his hand and then at him, and then back at the offered hand in confusion. "Come now." He waved his fingers in a welcoming gesture. She accepted his offer, and he guided her to the door where there hung a picture of two old people standing in front of a white house with big windows. The man wore eyeglasses and held a pitchfork, and the woman looked upset, like she would rather be doing something else. She liked the picture. They were the only other old people she knew other than the Dean. Everyone else was dead.

"Have Ruth give you two servings' worth like the others. And have a glass of mead as well," he told her as she opened the door to leave. She turned to thank him when he unexpectedly asked her, "You aren't leaving anything out, are you?"

She looked up into those gray eyes. "No, sir. Nothing," she promised.

"Good night," he told her, and she left to the kitchen in a hurry, making sure to lock the door behind her.

CHAPTER 5

The Tale Continues

The lock to the door clicked, and the Dean smiled at the picture. "Your painting still survives, Mr. Wood," he stated with pride, briefly recalling how the modernist masterpiece came into his possession, and then he spun on his heels, remembering his business with the bookshelf. Placing his hands on his hips, he studied the shelves and then began pulling out books at random, reading the fading titles and shoving them back restlessly. Dust kicked up and drifted into his face, causing him to sneeze several times. "Where are they?" he asked impatiently while wiping his nose with an aged silk handkerchief and then looking to his right at another bookshelf that was slightly taller than the first. Glancing up at the top of the other shelf, he spotted what he was looking for sitting among various trinkets and stacks of books placed randomly about. "Aha! There they are." He stood on his tiptoes and reached up for two books resting diagonally against a stack of a well-read collection of Tarzan paperbacks. One of the items resembled a pamphlet more than a book, and the other was a leather-bound tome that could have been centuries old. He brought them down from the shelf and gingerly brushed the dust off with the silk handkerchief.

The books lay in front of him, sitting next to the ashtray and pipe as he sat at his desk, staring at them. He opened the lower left-hand drawer, moved aside some miscellaneous items, and uncovered a bottle with a peeling black label. He opened the bottle and took a considerable swig and returned it to its hiding place. "Ahh. The good stuff," he said, letting the warm liquid paint his throat and then refocused on the books.

Softly running his hands on the leather book, he turned it so he could read its title, *De Graecorum Hodie Quorundum Opinationibus.* He whispered the translation to himself, "On the Belief of Some Greeks Today." He opened the book and flipped through the pages, very cautiously using only his fingernails until he located the passage he was looking for. "The Vrykolakas is the body of a man of wicked and debauched life, very often of one who has been excommunicated by his bishop. Such bodies do not like other corpses suffer decomposition after burial nor fall to dust..." The passage went on to describe a parched-skinned demon with extruding bones and the power to kill its victims without making contact. He continued to read, but the information wasn't quite what he was looking for, so he closed the book and set it aside with care.

Then he slid the pamphlet toward him. It was a black-and-white publishing from 1845, with an illustration of a caped skeleton hovering over a prone, unconscious woman wearing a gown. There was faded but still legible lettering above and below the illustration that read, *Varney the Vampire or Feast of Blood.* He considered the cover art and grinned as he pondered how the image grotesquely resembled Sleeping Beauty with one exception. In the cover art, the Prince Charming appeared to be risen from the dead. His grin fell short when he realized the irony, and an image of parading decomposing humans replaced his thoughts.

He twisted the cap back onto the black-labeled bottle after another generous swig and put it back in the desk drawer. "An overlooked literary classic," he said with a tipsy smile as he turned the thin cover page of the pamphlet open and settled into his reading. He didn't have long to read when he came across a passage in chapter one that read, "Each limb seems weighed down by tons of lead—she can but in a hoarse, faint-whispered cry..." These words quickly brought to his mind Gina's distant behavior and her strange whispering during their conversation. A little further in the same chapter, another passage caught his eye: "The figure turns half around, and the light falls upon the face. It is perfectly white—perfectly bloodless. The eyes look like polished tin…" It was very similar to Gina's description of the visitor, which is what initially caught The Dean's interest and gave him the inclination that their current guests were something of interest. At least one of them.

*****

"Hello," Gina hailed, as she entered the kitchen searching for Ruth. The odor of the night's supper still lingered in the air, and it set her salivary glands into overdrive. She noticed some bubbling pots on the stove and headed straight for them. She lifted one of the lids and quickly set it back with a clang. "Ouch!" she hissed while wildly shaking her hand in the air to cool it off.

"How many times are you gonna burn your fingers before you learn what a potholder is, girl?" Ruth scolded Gina as she stepped out from behind a pantry shelf, wiping away grease from her mouth with a soiled dish towel. Her black hair was tied up now, but several locks still managed to hang in front of her face, blocking her eyes.

"I was getting worried about you," she said while brushing her hair aside in vain as it dropped back in front of her face once she lowered her hand. "Frederick and Timothy just left. They couldn't stop talking about your mission up top," she continued while grabbing a plate from a shelf. Her assistant was slouching on a wooden chair in the corner, snoring. His oversized apron acting as a blanket.

"Dummies," Gina said as she pulled out a stool from under a table. "The Dean won't like that."

"I kinda had a feeling, so I made sure to remind them," Ruth explained as she walked up to Gina and handed her the plate, now piled high with stew, corn bread, and fruit. "They didn't like it. Especially Timothy, but they got the message."

Gina's eyes widened at the sight of the plate, and she thanked Ruth for the food and for dealing with Timothy and Frederick. As soon as she finished her plate, Ruth appeared with a piece of strawberry shortcake and set it next to Gina. After removing Gina's plate, she returned and pulled out the stool and sat next to her as she savored the shortcake.

"Good? I made it yesterday," Ruth whispered. "But don't tell the Dean. I didn't give him any," she added with a mischievous look that was partially hidden by her black hair.

"It's delicious," Gina replied.

Gina was removing whipped cream from her fork, relishing every bit of the sweet softness that hid in between the tines, when she noticed that Ruth was patiently sitting next to her, taking small sips from a teacup she held in front of her. She set the fork down on the plate amid the crumbs of the shortcake and turned to Ruth.

"What?" she asked in irritation.

Ruth gave her a sheepish grin and shrugged her shoulders as she took another sip of whatever she was drinking, with opal eyes peering over the cup directly at Gina.

"You know I can't tell you," Gina said.

"Come on. No one else is around," Ruth pleaded with her and looked in the corner at the snoring boy. "And Billy is out for the night. You can trust me, Gina. Besides, the boys practically spilled the beans already," she pointed out and took another sip from her cup.

Gina picked up the plate and licked it clean of its remaining crumbs like a cat. After which, she handed the plate over to Ruth, along with a suspicious look, before giving in. "Okay," she said with an exasperated sigh.

Ruth sat stoically on her stool as Gina poured out the details of the night's events. She told her of the fruit picker and how strange it was that he only took what he needed instead of hoarding the whole harvest the way the Dean said all strangers did. Ruth seemed bored with the discussion.

"I heard all of this from the boys," she said and drank from her cup again. This time it was more of a gulp that left a purple stain on her upper lip. "I wanna hear about the other one." Her dark eyes glowing more than usual.

Gina glanced at the cup in curiosity and gave Ruth a suspicious smile. She started the tale from when the other one climbed out of the bathroom window. As she described him, Ruth crept forward on her stool in eagerness, almost to the point of falling off. When she finished the story, Ruth was standing holding her cup and staring at Gina in amazement.

"What do you think it was?" she asked, lifting her cup to her purpled lips.

"What do you mean? He was a man. They were both men. At least they weren't the dead," Gina replied with a hint of doubt in her voicee as if she were trying to convince herself she was right.

Ruth continued to stare at Gina with docile, glassy eyes, not saying a word.

"What? I mean, he was a little weird. But we were tired, and it was dark. Our eyes could have been playing tricks on us," Gina said aloud, still trying to convince herself that she was right.

Ruth continued to stare in silence. Gina looked at her feet, feeling like she was hiding something from Ruth. She had a gift of getting information out of people without saying a word herself.

"There was something I didn't tell the Dean," she said with nervous apprehension.

Ruth pulled her stool closer to Gina and took a seat again, leaving her cup on the table. "What?"

Gina looked Ruth directly in the eyes, considering if she can trust her. "When he looked at us in the shoe, he talked to us. Or to me," she whispered and then paused.

"Tell me," Ruth whispered in return, putting a hand on Gina's knee.

"When he looked in our direction, I could hear him. He said, 'children.'" Gina's expression grew distant, and now she was staring through Ruth and not at her. Ruth noticed and shook her knee to snap her out of it, but all she offered was a blank stare. "And I could hear his whisper when I was with the Dean. 'Children,' he whispered to me again.'"

*****

Varick paused and looked around the area for a possible view outside in an attempt to judge the time. Henry noticed and pulled his silver watch out from his front pants pocket. "It's 1:48 a.m.," he said aloud. Varick looked down at Henry and thanked him. He stood up sometime ago to stretch his legs and had been pacing the room, narrating his tale to Henry for the past few hours. He decided sitting would be good again, so he sat on the floor with his back resting to the wall before he continued speaking.

Henry turned to lay on his back using a crumpled tablecloth as a pillow and closed his eyes. "Are you going to fall asleep on me? After all your grief?" Varick asked him when he noticed how comfortable Henry was making himself. "Don't worry. I'm listening. You were about to tell me about a trip to Europe," Henry said with confidence.

"Correct. But in order to understand the significance of the summer trip, you must first understand the world in which Ms. Borden was immediately surrounded and her sensibilities. Her family's roots and reputation were a birthmark that anyone would be proud to bear. However, she viewed it as a stain because of the inequality and poverty she witnessed when doing evangelical work in the tenements of Americas cities. Like many of the women of her class, she enjoyed the privilege of their family's financial status, yet at the same time suffered oppression because of her gender. And some believe sexual orientation.

Although she and her sister, Emma, had their foot in the door of cosmopolitan society, Elizabeth was also a devout Christian and was considered quite the progressive because of her involvement with the temperance movement. Societal expectations and a strong belief in Christianity fed her aspirations to prove she was not just a pious Victorian woman, but also someone who was willing to fight evil at any and all costs.

In 1890, Elizabeth was about to be thirty years old while her sister was approaching her forties, and both were unmarried. Furthermore, Lizzie and Emma had shown no interest in trading their liberty for the simple company of a man. Therefore, suitors were few and far between. Their portion of the Fall River community viewed them as a pair of spinsters who were unfit for marriage and past their reproductive prime. Hence, useless for a proper society. Of course, Lizzie being the Christian that she was, never grew concerned about being judged by anyone other than God.

When she neared her thirtieth year, she was well aware that she was destined to be labeled as a spinster, and she welcomed it. Without a husband and children to tend to, she could dedicate her life to doing the Lord's work of freeing sinners from their vices and ridding the world of evil.

As mentioned, Lizzie had been doing evangelical work with her sister and other female members of the Central Congregational Church, which began in her teens. She also taught Sunday school at her church and conducted Bible-study classes on the weekends to immigrant children who couldn't possibly understand a word she was saying.

Yet Ms. Borden felt that the work she was doing was not enough and that all she and her companions were accomplishing was preaching to the choir. They needed to venture forth into the areas where society's decadence really needed to be addressed. Where the devil has his claim on men's souls.

Her campaign began with blocking the entrances of dance halls and taverns while scolding the local customers with fiery sermons in true temperance fashion. Eventually, the business community, with support from political leaders, demanded that Lizzy stop, so she took her campaign deeper into the muck where the dregs of humanity engaged in the worst sort of vices: sodomy, fornication and drug addiction.

This sent the ladies in the direction of the fringes of Fall River society; the tenement yards, harbors, brothels, and opium dens where the group commenced to frequent brothels and taking the names of all who entered to satisfy their carnal desires at the expense of the traumatized women who were manipulated into making a living peddling flesh. Policemen in the pockets of the local madams and pimps attempted to intimidate Lizzie and her company into submission, but the connections and pocketbooks of their highly respected families put an immediate end to that. Consequently, this semicarte blanche inspired the ladies to utilize a more aggressive approach, so they started infiltrating whorehouses scantily clad and forcibly interrupting customers in midcoitus. Leaving them hanging as it were.

The opium dens fared no better. The ladies would follow unsuspecting opium addicts to their untold locations and barge into the dens with a holy rage armed with axe handles and rolling pins, kicking subdued smokers in the ribs and face as they lay in a stupor with clouded eyes. Pipes were smashed and tables toppled. Followed by more physical assaults aimed at the Chinese proprietors. Some say that during their jubilant wrath, they could hear the righteous ladies making xenophobic statements such as "Go back home, coolie" and "Dog eaters," exposing their true blue-blood roots.

Eventually, word of the girls' activity spread throughout the area, and they began to build a reputation as defenders of the week and keepers of the faith. Crowds would follow Lizzie and her sister Emma when they were in town running errands, hoping to witness the next episode of chastising the wicked. Women whose husbands had been led astray by the temptations of vice would visit the girls and offer them gifts in exchange for the safe return of their wayward spouses. The next evening, Lizzie and the girls could be seen tramping through the street, pulling some poor sap they found in a bar or brothel by the ear, and guiding him home to his abandoned family, encouraged by constant kicks to his backside. They were building quite the fan base.

Yet after all their efforts, Lizzie and her group of courtesans still felt like they were counting grains of sand in the desert while a windstorm raged with fury around them. Especially in regard with the opium trade. This peculiar business funded the gambling houses, brothels, and of course supplied the dens scattered about the region. What needed to be done was to prevent the product from reaching its destinations, which meant taking the fight straight to the source fifty-two miles away in the harbors of Boston where the opium was being unloaded and distributed to the various dens in Chinatown and throughout the greater Massachusetts area, Fall River as well.

So they started to gather clues and information provided to them via the various gentlemen they accosted during their raids at local taverns and houses of vice in exchange for mercy and the relief that they won't be paraded down the main avenue in shame. This led to the discovery of the date and time of a very lucrative shipment arriving in Boston Harbor. Elizabeth and her courtesans devised an elaborate plan to raid the shipment and toss the opium overboard. It would be the Boston Tea Party all over again.

The day before the shipment was expected to arrive, Elizabeth and company visited Boston under the guise of attending a Bible study being held at Old North Church. The group rented a room along the boardwalk using unassumed names and spent the evening preparing for their raid. They intended on dressing as ladies of the night and infiltrating the harbor in the same way they had done with the brothels of Fall River. But this time each of them knew that the stakes were higher, and the casualties would be far more serious than a couple of addicts and brothel regulars. Yet their resolve was as strong as their faith in God, so neither of them thought of going home until the task was completed.

The ship docked late in the evening, just before midnight, when the city hands the reigns over to the pimps, the gamblers, and the drunks who howl at the moon alongside the tomcats searching for pussy. Hours after the pious citizens of the community have retreated to their homes to sup and sleep.

The city may have been empty, but the harbor was crowded with human traffic. Word had spread through the area that a major shipment was arriving, attracting opportunists of all sorts. The street dealers who bribe dockworkers as a guarantee that a barrel or two will fall off a truck, junkies hoping to find that sailor who pinches the stash and offers rock bottom prices, and ladies of the evening advertising their wares for the newly arrived mariners with money burning holes in their pockets. There were even a few food vendors and musicians playing to their hearts' content. The setting was perfect, and everyone roaming about was too preoccupied with their visions of grandeur that they hardly took notice of the six unfamiliar faces wearing frayed lace gowns stalking the area and slowly making their way to the ship, each from a different direction.

However, they weren't as undistinguished as they thought. One of the ladies, Bridget, the Bordens' housekeeper, was approached by a gentleman who showed a great interest in getting to know her more intimately if the price was right. She was the only Catholic among the group, and Irish to boot, which sometimes brought suspicion from her peers who were taught to never trust Papists and their popish ways.

She ignored his advances and attempted to pass him up when he grabbed her by the arm and turned her toward him. His greasy face smelled like stomach bile and cheap scotch. "You think you're too pretty for me?" he grunted and squeezed her body between him and a wooden support beam while pulling up the lace material of her dress along her leg. A stiff bulge met his hand when he got to his desired destination, and when he looked up in surprise into her stern eyes there was an ice pick being held to his Adam's apple.

"Walk away, and you will live to drink another day," she whispered in his ear. He pulled his hand away and walked backward in a drunken stupor, mumbling to himself until he disappeared into the atmosphere of scum. Lizzie's cohort then adjusted her gown as well as the wooden axe handle, meat cleaver, and butcher's knife that were concealed along her waist and crotch and continued the mission.

Lizzie and her courtesans inched closer to the ship, weaving their way through the various activities taking place while never taking their eyes away from the cargo waiting to be unloaded. They had to board the ship swiftly and throw the opium overboard before anyone realized what was happening. The ship's captain stood diligently near the tender platform, keeping an eye out for his contact while the crew loaded the barrels of opium onto a wooden pallet with a large rope net lying underneath. A pulley with a sturdy hook at the end swayed with the tiny ocean breeze above the pallet, awaiting its heavy load.

Lizzie approached the boarding plank, hiding her face behind a hand fan, and batting her eyelashes at the captain who, without hesitation, put his hand out in front of him just as she reached the ship's accessway. This was the signal for the others to act. The other five moved in and rushed the plank, lifting their frilly dresses to expose their calves while pretending to be overwhelmingly enamored with the sailors. The captain had not expected the force and determination of these lust-filled women and was pushed aside like an old newspaper, causing him to trip over himself and fall overboard into the water between the ship and the dock. The first mate jumped to help the captain while the rest of the crew continued to load the precious cargo onto the pallet, but their progress was soon interrupted by a group of women who began adorning them with words of affection and caresses.

The crew, anxious to finish the task at hand and engage in a little carnal knowledge and social drinking, resisted the advances of the women to the least of their abilities, until the captain reappeared on deck dripping wet and filled with rage.

He stared directly at Lizzie, who was facing him wrapped in a crew member's burly, hair-covered forearms both swaying to and fro to the melodies of the pier musicians.

"Remove these harlots from the ship now!" he yelled while stamping water out of his leather shoes. "We have work to do!" he said, scowling at the men with fire in his eyes before heading to the captain's quarters to change his clothes with the first mate following closely behind.

"Alright, ladies. You heard the capt'n," a tall crew member with no neck said as he was guiding one of the women toward the exit. That was when Lizzie tore away from her companion while pulling out an axe handle from under her dress. The other women did the same, leaving the men empty-handed and staring in shock at six women holding kitchen knives and meat cleavers. The hairy-armed one wanted to laugh—a bunch of girls with kitchen utensils—then it dawned upon him. "They're here for the shipment!"

The one with no neck jumped on top of the pallet and attached the pulley to the cargo net, ordering his mates to move fast. At that moment, the captain was reaching for the door to his quarters when he heard the cry. "Those bitches! Get my gun!" he ordered his first mate.

The loaded pallet began slowly lifting off the ship's deck, with No Neck standing on top. Emma spotted the crew member controlling the pulley and headed straight for him while Lizzie and the others were swinging wildly at the crewmen with all their energy. The crew retreated step-by-step in fear and confusion until a husky man missing his right ear grabbed one of Lizzie's associates' knife-wielding arm and slammed his hand into her nose, shattering the cartilage and sprinkling blood on his fist. He let go of her arm, and she fell to the floor, holding her face and screaming in agony as blood leaked though her fingers. "They're just girls. Come on, men!" he yelled in victory just before a meat cleaver hit the back of his skull, wiping the smile away from his face and spraying the crew with his blood. His body slumped to the floor, along with Lizzie, who was desperately trying to remove the cleaver from his skull like a sword from a stone. She had to put her foot on his neck and struggle for a second before it was yanked away. When it was finally pulled free, she stood up and found several of the crew members looking at her in fear as she stood over the earless man's body while blood spewed from his head. She leaned down to check on her friend. "Stay there," she told her.

Lizzie moved forward and the crew backed away from her like she was the devil. She ran toward the pulley that was now being steered toward the dock, with No Neck straddling the cargo. "Do not let that cargo reach the dock!" she yelled, but the other women were too occupied with the crew. She spotted Emma, and she was having trouble at the pulley gauge with an older crew member, who was reluctant to strike her. "Help, Emma," she ordered to anyone who could hear her through the commotion and continued to run toward the hanging cargo. No Neck, who was watching Lizzie very closely, observed the scene at the pulley gauge and urged the crew to assist the old man while he pulled a large knife out from under his wool-sweater vest, readying himself for a confrontation with one very angry lady.

A large crowd gathered in front of the ship as the action unfolded, which made it difficult for any support for the crew to reach the ship. They watched while the cargo made its way to the dock, with a tall man standing on top, screaming orders. As they were craning their necks looking up at the cargo, swinging over them, what appeared to be a bridesmaid jumped from the ship and grabbed on to the bottom of the cargo net, holding a meat cleaver in her mouth like a pirate. The crowd oohed at the sight and complained at the shoving of the henchmen breaking through the mob of people to assist with protecting the cargo.

No Neck's feet budged when something hit the cargo, and then he saw Lizzie clinging to the net, sweat-soaked hair sticking to her face as she grunted, trying to gain a foothold. He glanced down to measure the closing distance of the dock and saw the reinforcements arriving, which raised his spirits to no end. "Your too late, bitch. You and your sewing club are in for it now! Hahaha." He laughed and aimed his knife at the oncoming goons. Lizzie ignored him and continued to lift herself until her feet were firmly planted in the net.

Meanwhile, Emma was struggling with a gray-haired man who was doing his best to protect the pulley as much as possible without hitting her. He held her arms back with an iron grip, so she tried striking him with her knees in the groin, but he was swift in the hips for an old man and dodged every attempt. During their tussle, she caught sight of another crew member wearing a dark-blue sailor's beanie rushing toward them with a club in his hand. The old man noticed him too, and a large grin appeared on his face as he strengthened his grip on Emma when she desperately tried to pull away. "Be gentle with her, boy." He laughed as the sailor raised his hand to strike down on the bulging eyes of Emma. She was about to scream when the dark-blue beanie flew off the sailor's head accompanied by the sound of a baseball flying out of a ballpark.

The body was shoved forward and trampled over by a woman in a chiffon evening gown. Her auburn hair was kept in a long, thick braid that was coiled around her neck. She moved forward twirling a bloodied, wooden axe handle in her hands. The old man's eyes widened, and he let go of Emma and jumped overboard. "Hit the switch. Hurry!" the auburn-haired one ordered. Emma hit the pulley gauge, and it stopped right in midair.

No Neck's body jerked when the pulley abruptly stopped moving, and he grabbed the rope with both hands, almost dropping his knife. He looked toward the gauge and saw two lace-clad women fiddling with the pulley. Then he heard something from beneath him. "God, grant me the courage to act when necessary." It was Lizzie, and she was still holding on strong. She spotted the pulley and saw her sister and Felicity standing by the pulley gauge, debating about something. She knew they wouldn't be able to hear her from where they were, so she gave a high-pitched whistle like a cattle herder. The two quickly looked up and saw Lizzie climbing the side of the hanging cargo net with No Neck standing on top, holding a very large knife. They shrugged their shoulders and gave each other a questioning look right before hitting the pulley switch.

"No! Stop them!" No Neck screamed as the cargo began swinging back toward the ship.

At that moment, the ship's captain stormed the deck with a revolver in his hand aimed straight at the two women controlling the pulley. The first mate was right as his heels. He was poised to shoot when a pair of silk-hosen legs wrapped around his neck in a figure four and lifted him off the ground. He dropped his revolver and reached for his neck, attempting to break from the clutches of the silk-skinned boa constrictor.

"Oliver. Get the gun," he gasped.

The first mate hesitated in a panic and looked from the gun on the blood covered-deck floor to the captain, who was being carried away with the cargo by a…"Streetwalker?" The young man ran toward the tender and left the ship behind him, along with all his romantic notions of a smuggler's life. "There's no shame in being a clerk," he said to himself as he sped down the boardwalk to who knows where.

The cargo continued to swing outward toward the water with No Neck, Lizzie, and the captain in tow as a group of four henchmen landed on deck and headed toward the pulley gauge. The skirmish intensified, but the women would not let up. The henchmen moved forward, swinging their fists, and reaching for the women's weapons while Emma and Felicity maneuvered the cargo toward the ocean.

No Neck was about to jump from the cargo into the melee, but then he saw Lizzie still clinging to the net with the captain tied up in her legs. "Goddammit" was all he could say and began lowering himself to assist the captain.

The henchmen were pushing the women back closer to the pulley gauge, and the remaining crew members joined in with renewed vigor. Two crew members were anchoring the others and shoving them forward with words of encouragement and reminding everyone of the value of the cargo when one fell to the floor, holding his intestines in his hands, as a kitchen knife sliced across the neck of the other one, leaving him to swallow his words with blood. The henchmen looked back to see their mates squirming and kicking as a thin figure with a smashed nose and two black eyes walked over them while pulling a wooden club from under her gown.

"Just as sure as my name is Constance, so shall you suffer God's wrath!" was all the men heard before a windmill of blows rained down on them like an avalanche, while at the same time Bridget, Deborah, and a thin figure with pointy shoulders and light-brown hair charged from the flanks with meat cleavers swinging wildly.

The cargo was now over the water, and Lizzie's legs were cramping, so she dropped the captain into the harbor and turned up to see No Neck watching helplessly as the captain fell into the water, cursing up a storm. He continued lowering himself toward her with a murderous fury in his eyes that plainly said, "You fucking bitch!" And just as if she read his mind, he stated as much with the added threat, "You're mine." He wanted a fight, but she couldn't oblige him. Not tonight. Time was running short. He inched closer and started swinging his knife in her direction. She held tight to the meat cleaver and swung for his foot, and the cleaver landed in the cargo net right next to his toes.

"You missed, bitch," he taunted her when she pulled the cleaver from the rope, and his foot fell loose, making him lose hold of his knife as he reached for the net. *The bitch is going to cut the net*, he thought, and he yelled at the men to get the cargo back over the ship. Lizzie swung again at the net, and it opened a wide enough gap to allow a barrel of opium to squeeze through and fall into the water with a plop that was followed by other splashes as several people jumped from the dock to retrieve the barrel, each with their own personal interests in mind.

No Neck tried kicking her, and the cargo started spinning on its axis like a top in midair. The women gathered in front of the pulley control and kept the henchmen at bay while Lizzie continued to hack at the net until it opened like an angel's trumpet and released the cargo into the harbor waters, barrels dropping like a flurry of cannonballs accompanied by the rest of the crowd from the dock. Greedy cries of joy swam around in a confusing soup of opium barrels and wet clothes as the captain fought off the scavengers to get back at his ship.

Emma and Felicity heard the loud splash and looked to the pulley and saw the empty cargo net suspended over the water resembling a deflated balloon with Lizzie and No Neck hanging, legs kicking at each other.

"Swing it back this way," Felicity urged, and Emma hit the control lever, jerking the pulley back in the direction of the dock before destroying it with a wooden axe handle.

The henchmen and the women halted their struggle and gazed up as Lizzie and No Neck kept at their duel of legs while the pulley swung over the ship. They watched as Lizzie put her fingers to her mouth and blasted out another high-pitched whistle. The women let go of their weapons, pushed the men aside, and ran for the pulley, jumping for the dangling rope ends.

No Neck clung to the torn ropes, along with Lizzie and her entourage, who were staring daggers at him from all directions as the pulley swung to the dock. He looked to the ship and saw the men running from the ship to the dock, desperately trying to catch up with the female raiders, but it was too late. All was lost, and No Neck knew it. He also knew that there would be a heavy price to pay. He glared at Lizzie and let go of the ropes with a sigh and fell into the gloomy water at the edge of the approaching dock.

When the pulley was over the dock, Lizzie and her group leaped from the ropes and ran down the pier toward the main thoroughfare. They stopped at the cross-section and looked up and down the street, breathing heavily, each sweating through their gowns.

"Where are they?" Felicity asked between gritted teeth as she adjusted the thick braid of hair around her neck.

"Here they come," Bridget exclaimed, pointing at a vehicle floating on a dark cloud of dust approaching fast from the east.

A charcoal-black carriage with four thick-hooved Clydesdales attached to it was charging at them and came to a brisk halt inches away, kicking up pebbles and dust. There was a broad-shouldered woman with vein-filled hands that appeared strong enough to twist off the heads of ten chickens at once. She looked down at the women and grunted, and then the carriage door opened. Constance boarded, holding her nose, accompanied by Felicity and Emma. Lizzie ran around the front of the carriage and sat next to the driver while Bridget and Deborah rode on the side of the carriage, clinging to the railing.

The black carriage raced out of Boston Harbor straight toward the railway station, kicking up pebbles as it passed policemen on horseback and afoot, headed in the other direction.

CHAPTER 6

Consequences

Varick opened his eyes and took a deep breath. Henry was still lying on the floor, but he was up on one elbow again, shaking his head slowly, looking very entertained.

"How come I haven't heard any of this before? It's good stuff," he asked.

"That's because Elizabeth Borden's life, and those around her, have been intentionally shrouded in legend and mystery, and not without reason. The individuals and entities in power made sure that none of this was recorded or remembered in order to maintain their status and the economic and social structure." Varick's eyes tightened in anger when he made this last statement.

"Hmm?" Henry queried as he adjusted his body into a more comfortable position, preparing to hear more.

"However, I can attest to a certain degree, that this incident did indeed take place," said Varick. "If you recall, I mentioned that I was returning to the States from Europe around the same time Ms. Borden and her company were coming home from their own European excursion." He looked to Henry, who nodded his head in recognition.

"Prior to my departure," he continued, "I leisured in Boston for a spell and was taking residence at a well-known establishment on School Street that was located roughly six miles above the harbor, the Parker House. During this time, the hotel was building a reputation as a haven for travelers and locals who had an acquired taste for some of the finer amenities in life. As well as the many vices their station and money could buy. The usual roster of guests consisted of judges, politicians, police commissioners, bankers, and real estate investors each accompanied with a voluptuous vixen whom they all referred to as their assistant.

"It was rather cool that evening as the trade winds coming from the ocean stirred the air, and I remember sitting at the hotel bar enjoying a glass of a vintage 1865 Don Pedro Madeira in anticipation of a delicious meal out in the city. Boston's finest." His lips parted, and he exhaled in reminiscence as visions of crystal chandeliers, velvet curtains, and men in tailcoats carrying gold-tipped canes hovered in front of him like dancing phantoms in a haunted house.

"My mind and appetite were occupied with thoughts of warm blood and tender flesh when the barkeep asked if I wanted another glass. Before I could respond, a woman's voice spoke, 'Of course he will. And make it two.'"

Varick turned toward the voice to see who it belonged to, and there was a wire-waisted female with slender pointy shoulders, wearing a deep red sleeveless evening dress made of silk that flowed over her hips and bunched at the floor behind a pair of cream-colored ankles in heeled shoes as red as the dress. She batted her eyes and her long, false eyelashes moved like peacock feathers.

He was aware of her presence before she spoke as her overwhelming odor arrived half a minute in advance. The fragrance was French and expensive, most likely a gift from her "employer," but it was quite apparent that she had no knowledge of the concept of moderation. An indication that she was nothing more than a common trollop adorned in the wages of the paramour.

She held her hand out to Varick and introduced herself. "Bonsoir. Ms. Collins. And you are?"

Varick rose from his barstool and nodded his head in recognition while reaching out for her hand. "Bonsoir, mademoiselle. Varick. Charmed, I'm sure," he replied as he brought her hand toward his mouth. The veins on the back of her hand cried out to him as the fresh, green fluid not yet exposed to oxygen pulsed underneath her pale, perfumed skin. He gave her a peck on the hand and hesitated before letting it go.

The bartender arrived with their drinks and set the two wine goblets on the bar in front of them. Varick told the barkeep to bill his suite as he waved his hand toward the empty barstool next to his, and they both took a seat. They touched glasses and took a sip. The woman's eyes squinted, and she puckered her lips. "A bit dry, isn't it?"

"It's a Sercial from Madeira." He told her. They're made to be especially dry. It's an acquired taste." He watched her with a wary eye and a smile as she took another drink and feigned enjoyment.

She set her glass down and put her hand on Varick's, offering him a flirtatious look. "Varick, is it? What an interesting name? An interesting name for an interesting man." She continued with the pleasantries for a while and stated that her first name was Alexis. Varick looked at her, saying nothing, and raised his glass to his mouth.

"Mysterious too," she whispered enticingly, while gently rubbing his hand.

He remained silent and gulped down the last portion of his wine and gestured for the barkeep. He removed his hand from hers and reached for his waist coat pocket and pulled out a money clip and left a few notes on the bar as a tip. Alexis glanced at the bills and back at Varick with a pouty look on her face. "Aww. Does that mean you're leaving? We just met, Varick." She stood from her stool and drew near him, close enough for him to feel the warmth of her body radiating from underneath her red dress. He was growing tired of her presence as his only desire was to feed, and she was hindering his ability to satiate himself. *Damn woman*, he thought.

He made eye contact with her and moved closer. They stared into each other's eyes, with only their breath separating them. She blinked seductively, and Varick could hear her false eyelashes clash together like thunder and see microscopic flakes of eye makeup drift in the air around her nose until they settled in her pores.

"Shouldn't I be concerned?" he asked her.

"About what?" she replied innocently.

"About your employer," he said dryly. He stressed the word *employer* and accompanied it with a raised eyebrow, giving the implication that he was savvy with the arrangement.

She took a step back and with jaw agape placed her palms on her chest appearing to be insulted. *Very well"* he thought. Now maybe she would go about her business, and he could be about his.

He stood up to leave, but she blocked his way and gingerly grabbed him by the lapels of his jacket. "I have no employer, and I'm here all alone," she whined to him while she smoothed the lapels with her palms. He looked at her with suspicion in his eyes while she explained that she was recently fired by her employer on account of his wife showing up unexpectedly at the hotel last night and discovering her in his room.

"How very unfortunate," Varick sympathized while she continued to rub her palms over his jacket.

"Isn't it? And now I'm here all alone with no place to go once I check out of the hotel," she purred into his ear.

He grabbed her hands and lowered them to her side as their eyes locked in anticipation. His hunger was increasing, and the moon was moving closer to the horizon. Maybe he would have to opt for eating in after all. He raised his hand and stroked her along her right ear, until he reached the soft flesh behind her earlobe just between the jawbone and cranium. She leaned closer to his touch, and he decided that he would dine in for the night.

"Have you eaten dinner yet?" he asked.

Her eyes lit up, and she stated that she was famished. He offered her his arm, and she slipped hers around it. "As am I. I hear they serve a delicious prime rib. Extra rare," he said while he guided her out of the bar. "Perhaps afterward we can take a walk in the garden and bask in the moonlight."

"Sounds wonderful," she replied, seeming very pleased.

As Varick walked with her, the veins in her neck called out to him, and her overwhelming fragrance seemed to disappear. He was pleased as well. "Maybe we should enjoy the garden before we dine?" he suggested.

"How romantic," she exclaimed.

As they were exiting the bar, a young man wearing a dark-gray wool vest over a long-sleeved, white cotton shirt and a pair of brown trousers was shoving his way through the lobby crowd and heading toward the bar. He bumped into Varick as he passed through, making his way to a table where three well-dressed older gentlemen sat drinking cognac. He stood in front of their table quietly, nervously wringing a black hat in his hands.

The three were laughing at someone else's misfortune, when one of them with thick silver sideburns exhaled a cloud of pipe smoke and looked up at the man and asked him what he wanted. "Don't just stand there, young man. Out with it."

The man hesitated and dropped his hands to his side before speaking. "There is a raid at the docks, and the shipment is being thrown overboard." He explained while looking down in shame. The other two silver-haired gentlemen did not react. They discreetly rose from their seats and left the area, leaving Silver Chops to deal with the dilemma. The young man bowed his head to the two gentlemen as they departed.

Silver Chops leaned forward on a cane that he was holding and glared bullets at the young man. "What do you mean there was a raid?" he growled.

"A gang of whores raided the docks, and they're throwing the shipment overboard," the young man blurted out. By this time, everyone in the bar was focusing their attention on the two at the table, so Varick took the opportunity to slip out of the room unnoticed and head for the roof.

*****

Henry was standing up, stretching his legs, and looking at his pocket watch while Varick continued with the tale. It was approaching 4:00 a.m. and he hadn't slept a wink yet, but the story was too good to miss. It was one of Varick's best thus far.

Varick noticed Henry examining his watch and asked the time. Henry told him, and Varick nodded in acknowledgement while he went on with the tale.

"The reason I headed for the roof was to see if I could catch a glance of the action at the harbor six miles away. From that perspective, I could see a great commotion and hear the screams of the people involved. Some were cries of rage, while others were exclamations of joy and surprise. My enhanced senses permitted me to witness the tumult as if it were happening across the avenue, and I could see evening gowns flowing like sails darting across the ship while burly sailors appeared to be tripping over their own feet, and in the background there were splashes like cannonballs as barrels fell into the ocean water.

"When I was about to return to the bar, I overheard the other hotel guests, including Silver Chops and the young man, gathered on the second-floor terrace. I peeked over the side of the roof, and I saw them straining their eyes in an attempt to view the raid. Silver chops was holding a small telescope to his eye while cursing at the young man."

"Where in the hell is Barrett? What are we paying that thick-necked fool for?" He looked at the young man, who shrugged his shoulders, still wringing his hat when he was shoved out of the way by a sweaty, potbellied man who was buttoning his shirt and adjusting his jacket. A police commissioner's coat.

"What the fuck is this about a raid?"

Silver Chops snapped at him. "You tell me, O'Brien. I thought you had this type of thing under control. I suggest you get your arse out there fast and stop those bitches before you're replaced." The commissioner stepped toward Silver Chops but thought better of it and left calling after several men to follow him. Other officers who were wetting their tongue at the hotel while their wives supped alone.

The crowd at the dock was still roaring with enthusiasm while I observed the scene from the roof. However, I soon lost interest as my hunger was distracting me. That was when I remembered Ms. Collins. "Where had she gone off to?" I asked myself. I turned to make my way back into the hotel, hoping that she was still available for dinner when the rumblings of a horse-drawn carriage caught my attention. I looked to my right and glimpsed the tail end of a carriage racing down Washington Street toward the downtown area, with two women desperately hanging on to the luggage railings. "Ride like the wind," I whispered after them as they made their escape. I recall smiling to myself at the image of O'Brien and his "Keystone Cops" bumbling their way to the scene of the crime a day late and a dollar short. Little did I know that this particular group of ladies would eventually become the scourge of vampires along the Eastern Seaboard.

And then a soft voice called out from behind the hotel where the garden was located: "Varick, Varick. Where are you, my dear?" I looked to the sky and inhaled the rays of the moon as silver-gray clouds brushed across its face. "Coming, my dear."

*****

"Varick?" Alexis stood under an elm tree, shaded from the moonlight and garden lanterns, trying to make sense of the shadows. "Darn. I guess I'll be dining alone," she sadly exclaimed and started for the hotel.

Varick landed behind her as soft as a falling leaf. He straightened his coat and collar. "There you are. I thought I'd lost you," he said slyly while swallowing the rush of saliva that flooded his mouth like a hungry wolf.

"You startled me," she declared with a hand over her heart.

"My apologies. I promise that will never happen again," he told her while offering his arm.

"As long as you promise. I'm hungry," she purred while allowing him to guide her.

"Indeed," he said. "But first. Have you ever heard of the corpse flower?"

"No," she replied.

"Well, there is a spectacular specimen here. They keep it in the back because of its rarity. It only blooms every seven to ten years," he explained. "They're quite a sight."

"Sounds fascinating. And then we can eat?" she asked.

"Yes. Then we will eat," he assured her while eyeing her pale-skinned shoulders and guiding her to a very dark recess of the hotel garden.

*****

"So you ate her?" Henry asked with a curled lip.

"I don't eat people. I am not a cannibal," Varick explained.

"Well then, you drank her blood," Henry stated.

Varick stared bullets at him and sighed in frustration, and possibly weariness. It was well after 4:00 a.m., and henry was showing no signs of letting up. He wanted to hear it all, so he continued.

*****

The raid immediately caught the attention of the Fall River elites, whose investments were being disrupted by Lizzie's group, and they demanded it be stopped. Cursing drunks and preaching to whores was one thing, but interfering with the ebb and flow of their financial system would not be tolerated. It was no secret that much of the old money in Massachusetts, including fall River, was a consequence of the early merchant class participating in the illegal opium trade in China. Their dirty money was the lifeblood that kept their illustrious society afloat. Furthermore, after the Civil War, a wave of addiction swept across the United States as soldiers returned home with the taste of morphine in their veins and the everlasting memories of shattered limbs and exploding brains. As a result, the same Massachusetts merchants continued to increase their opium profits with the new homegrown market, while at the same time pointing the finger of blame in the direction of Chinatown. These unethical business ventures were overlooked by the virtuous Victorian community so long as the problem was contained to certain areas, and because they often funded the hospitals, schools, and commerce in general.

This was a serious offense that had to be dealt with swiftly and with a certain amount of brutality to serve as a lesson to others who would dare make such a move against them. If word got out that a bunch of wagtails got the upper hand on them, then what would be next. Children? No, this mysterious group of women have been creating havoc in Fall River, and now it appeared that they were bringing their affairs to Boston. There was a heavy price to pay, and the first step in redeeming payment was to identify who these women were.

This was a job for professionals. Mercenaries. A few hardened, battle-worn veterans would do the job. Word was spread throughout the taverns and brothels in the area that Silver Chops was looking for a few good men. By this time news of the raid had spread, so it was no mystery as to what the task may entail, which immediately attracted the best of the worst: Indian killers, former Pinkertons, independent ranch hands from out West, and the like.

Silver Chops was staring at the three men standing on the other side of his English oak desk, trying to conceal his contempt. They were exactly what he requested, hardened soldiers with experience in the battlefield, and according to their testimonies these three Indian War veterans fit the bill to a tee. Ruthless, cunning, and available for the right price. However, their hygiene and manner desperately needed improving. This opinion was reinforced when the one on the left turned and spit on his polished wooden floors. The scar on the side of his mouth gave him the appearance of having a permanent smile.

"A bunch of whores from Fall River, you say?" the middle one asked gruffly. He displayed a grimy smile filled with crooked, plaque-coated, dark-yellow teeth bordering on orange. "Funny," he went on, "I was in that town about a month back, and I heard rumors of a group of holy-roller maidens that were making the husbands of the city shake in their boots. Could it be that these are the one and same that interfered with your shipment?" He sucked on his yellow teeth as he tapped his belt buckle with is thumb. It was a large buckle made of deer horn with a woven, silky-black lining around the edge that may have been human hair.

"We believe so," Silver Chops answered as he leaned back in his leather chair with hands folded in front of his chin. "The task is a simple locate and eliminate that shouldn't be too difficult. After all, they're women."

"That's probably what your crew thought too?" Yellow Teeth stated flatly while examining Silver Chops from above.

Silver Chops glared at him for a moment. "That's why you three are here. Right?"

Yellow Teeth nodded in agreement. "What about payment?

Silver Chops turned in his chair and grabbed a canvas bag lying on a bookshelf behind him. He tossed the bag on the desk, and it slid across the smooth finish toward the edge of the desk. The one standing to the right of Yellow Teeth reached out and caught the bag before it hit the floor. Silver Chops was impressed by his catlike reflexes straight out of an Old West serial and was assured that he had hired the right men for the job.

"There's half. The other half will be yours once the task is complete," Silver Chops explained to them. "And remember, gentlemen, we want proof."

The three nodded in unison. It was a basic agreement with no reason to gripe, and all three were anxious to leave the company of Silver Chops, so they could settle their tabs at the various bars, brothels, and bathhouses throughout the city before moving out.

*****

Seven days later, a haggard-looking individual walked into Amrhein's Tavern on West Broadway and ordered a whiskey from the bar. The daytime regulars paid him no mind until his odor entered their mouths. The bartender kept a safe distance and cautiously slid the drink toward the man. He gulped down the high-proof elixir without flinching and set the glass on the bar without comment. His fingers were encrusted with dried blood, as was his face, preventing anyone from recognizing him. His clothes were tattered and covered in filth, and he wore only one boot.

"That'll be five cents, sir," the bartender apprehensively demanded while feeling the back pocket of his trousers for his one-shot Derringer.

The man collapsed. His chin hit the bar on the way down, snapping his head back and causing him to fall backward. He awoke the next morning covered with a multicolored quilt and lying on a wool mattress. After he cleared the gooey clouds from his eyes, he noticed that he was in a small bedroom with a square window curtained in gray linen. There was a nightstand with a pitcher of water and an upside-down glass on it next to the bed, and an armchair with a set of clean clothing resting over the back. Underneath the chair was a pair of modest-looking brown leather shoes.

A small knock sounded at the door before opening. "Oh. Good, you're awake. Mr. Cross would like to see you as soon as your available." It was an older heavyset woman wearing a light-blue dress under a white apron. Her silver-streaked hair was tied up in a loose bun, leaving a few strands to hang over her forehead and ears. "And I could use this room for paying customers." She stressed this last statement by gathering the bedding that he was still lying under.

He sat up in the bed and turned to stand while she worked around him. Extreme pain rushed to his skull and every other bone in his body as soon as he rose to his feet. He examined himself and saw that other than the spotted bandages on his ribs and hands, he was naked.

The woman took notice of his confusion. "Don't worry. Your chastity is still intact," she said mockingly.

"Where am I?" He grimaced in pain.

"Upstairs from the tavern. Now hurry along. You shouldn't keep Mr. Cross waiting." She held the bedding in her arms and grabbed the water pitcher before exiting the room.

His entire body ached, and his legs wanted to melt beneath him as he stood in front of Mr. Cross, sweating profusely. He was wearing the navy-blue trousers and beige linen shirt that were provided him. The shirt was showing signs of blood along the sides where his bandages needed to be changed and dressed. Everything fit well more or less, except the shoes, which were rather snug because of his feet being swollen because of the long trek from Fall River. He pulled out a handkerchief from his back pocket and dabbed his forehead and then wiped the scar that ran from his mouth to his cheekbone.

Mr. Cross sat in disbelief while the man with the scar described the incidents that resulted in the death of his two companions. His eyes tightened in suspicion, and his silver sideburns squirmed like white caterpillars as he chewed on the stem of his pipe while the man with the scar gave what details he could recall of the mission. The man's hands trembled with terror and rage, and his chin quivered as if a phantom suddenly appeared behind Silver Chops.

"Get it together, man," Silver Chops urged him as he offered him a drink and a seat. "Just tell me what happened."

He took a large gulp and held the crystal goblet close to his chest like a security blanket. "We were made as soon as we arrived. They led us around like sheep, and we played right into their hands. The townsfolk were cooperative, especially the women, and they told us everything we wanted to know about the group. Or at least what they wanted us to know. The community pretended that they were at odds with the group and made us believe that they wanted to be rid of them. We observed their comings and goings for some days and got a chance to witness their works firsthand when they protested a tavern that we were using as our base of operations. It turns out they were using the event to recon the establishment and make a positive ID of their targets. Us.

"On the day we were going to carry out and complete the mission, the mood seemed different. The townsfolk were extra nice, yet there were fewer of them roaming about the area. We had information that the group of ladies gathered at an abandoned barn on the edge of the city every Thursday afternoon after choir practice. The plan was to surround the perimeter, lock them in, and torch the place to make it look like an unfortunate accident. No one would be the wiser.

"We sat in wait, strategically positioned around the barn the entire day until they arrived. The first three showed up together, strolling along the dirt path that led to the barn, each wearing oversized straw hats that shaded their faces. A quarter of an hour had passed when others began to appear individually on the same path about five minutes apart, all wearing the same type of oversized hat. Eleven in all. Once they were inside, there wasn't much activity other than small chatter.

"We lay in five feet of wild grass, waiting to make our move. Brett and Miguel were to crawl in real slow to bolt the front and back entryways, and once they gave the signal, I was supposed to set fire to the surrounding brush. After the fire was set, we would shoot anyone that was lucky enough to make it out alive. But that never happened.

"I was squatting behind a boulder surrounded by long grass, waiting for the signal, when the chatter from inside the barn grew louder. Brett and Migs were taking too long, so I gave the familiar bird whistle as a sign that I was in position. There was no response other than more chatter from inside the barn, mixed with small bursts of laughter. Something was wrong. I crawled to the spot where Brett should have been waiting, and there was no sign of him other than the imprint of flat grass where he was lying. *Shit!* I thought. They were on the move, and I wasn't in position. I started to scramble back to my point when I heard Brett groaning from inside the barn, 'Rot in hell, you bitches!' There was more laughter.

I crept up to the barn and peeked through a small crack in the wood, and they had Migs and Brett hanging from support columns with their hands and feet tied behind them. There was a third column with iron railroad spikes hammered into it a few feet away. They knew we would be there and exactly where to find us. I made fast for the boulder, and there was a lady sitting on top of it with legs crossed, fanning herself with an oversized hat. She looked in my direction and blew a kiss.

"The pain in my head is what opened my eyes, and I was hanging from the column next to the bloodied Migs and Brett. Migs was gritting his teeth, the ones they hadn't pulled out yet, and glaring at the redhead in front of him while she slid a bougainvillea thorn under his index fingernail. I looked over at Brett to check out his condition, and he looked like he had been put through the wringer. He hung there with his chin clinging to his chest, exhaling blood and spit. His face was beat to a pulp, and each time he struggled to breath his lungs would whistle.

"The redhead backed away from Migs. 'This one has a lot to repent for. I can see it in his eyes.' After she said this, a dark-haired woman with gray eyes rose from a bale of hay and walked up to Migs.

"'We know who sent you, so don't bother with your lies,' she lectured. 'Your only choice now is to repent for your sins and life of vice,' she continued as she paced before all three of the hanging men. She stopped in front of Brett and lifted his head with the handle of a butcher knife she was holding, so she could look in to his purpled, puffy face. His right eye was one blink away from popping out of its socket. "You wouldn't want to meet the Creator with a guilty conscience now, would you?" She moved the handle, and his chin fell to his chest, and the eyeball hung by a string.

"She twirled the knife around in her hand and returned to Migs. 'Do you have anything to repent?" she asked him. All he had to offer was silence and defiance. She returned to her seat on the haystack. 'These men and their pride,' she said, nodding in disappointment. 'What do you suggest, Maggie?'

"'A little taste of the leather should open his heart to God.' The reply was painted in a thick Irish accent. A stout brunette with a long face and dark eyes stepped out from the lengthening shadows of sunset and approached Migs as she unclipped a bullwhip from her belt that she wore like a sash. She snapped the whip in the air and began to recite the Act of Contrition. 'Oh my God…' *Crack!* 'I'm heartily sorry…' *Crack!* 'For having…' *Crack!* 'Offended thee…' *Crack!*

"Her rage-filled prayer went on for about five minutes, and with each snap of the whip drops of Migs's blood landed on my face. When she finished, she made the sign of the cross and returned to the shadows. There were small grumblings from the other ladies aimed at her gestures, and I could hear one of them hiss the word: 'Catholics.'

"By that time, I was soaked in Migs's blood and my own piss. The one sitting on the haystack stood and walked outside without saying a word, and the others followed without question. She was the leader. A thick, liquid-filled cough from Migs caught my attention, and when I looked his way, I lost what was left in my stomach.

"His clothing and skin had been torn to shreds by the handy whip work of the Irish woman. His body was covered in so much blood that it was hard to make out which tears and flaps were skin, and which were clothing. The skin on his face was barely hanging on to the surviving muscle tissue, and his eyeballs were reeling around in their sockets. He tried to make eye contact with me, but his eyes wouldn't obey, and his detached lips moved under his chin bone as if he had something to say. "'Repent,' I whispered to him before he stopped moving completely. They were both seconds away from death, and their shit-stained pants were starting to attract flies.

"The ladies returned, and all of them surrounded me, but only the leader spoke. 'You will deliver a message for us,' she started as one of the women was cutting the rope around my hands and feet. I fell to the floor and brought myself up on my hands and knees, when a foot pushed me back down. 'Tell Mr. Cross that the time has come for he and his friends to atone for their sins.' After her statement, she turned and walked out of the building, and the other women began beating me with wooden clubs. When they were done giving me the once-over, they dragged me out of the barn and held my face up and forced me to watch them burn it down with Migs and Brett still inside."

"Don't forget the message," the Irish one scolded, and then they were gone with only the echo of their singing voices trailing behind, "God is trying to tell you something…"

*****

Silver Chops eased back in his chair and took a draw from his pipe as he watched the man in front of him wipe tears from his face. This same man who had once given the impression of a stone-cold killer was now sitting here hugging his glass and whimpering like a little girl. "Tell me then, who is this leader?"

The man wiped a tear away and took another sip of his drink without looking up at Mr. Cross. "I heard them call her Lizzie. But the Irish one called her Ms. Borden."

Silver Chops' white eyebrows raised at the mention of the name. He set his pipe down and cleared his throat. "Are you certain?" he asked.

"Yes. There were two of them. The Irishwoman called them both Ms. Borden," he explained while staring at the bottom of his glass "Lizzie and… Emma. The older one's name was Emma."

A brown canvas bag landed on top of the desk. The man's eyes drifted to the desk and back to his glass. "No, I can't take that," he mumbled while shaking his head.

Mr. Cross walked around the desk, picked up the bag, and handed it to the man. "Take it," he told him. "Go somewhere peaceful."

He sat behind his desk sipping scotch and going over the recent information in his mind. The Borden name was very familiar to him, but these ladies couldn't possibly be connected to the Bordens of Fall River. "Or could they be?" he wondered. Andrew's first wife did provide him with daughters, and they would be well into adulthood by now. This was quite a perplexing development, and because of the individuals involved, the situation was delicate and would take some personal looking into as well as a visit to Fall River. He yelled out to his secretary, "Agnus! Clear my calendar for tomorrow. I'll be having lunch in Fall River."

CHAPTER 7

Europe

The patriarchs of Fall River's most prominent families were gathered in the upstairs boardroom of the local lumber and coal company, discussing the recent meeting they had with their friend from Boston. A very heated discussion. Andrew Borden, who was among them, was the unfortunate focus of the gathering.

"Those daughters of yours are ruining our relationship with Boston, man. Along with that Irish foreigner who you've hired as a housekeeper," expressed an individual who was staring daggers at Andrew. He had a thick handlebar mustache that wiggled under his nose when he spoke.

"Enough bickering! Besides, I believe your daughters were a part of this fiasco too, Mr. Brayton," said a man who was sitting at the head of the table. "Everyone here knows your daughters are the best of friends with the Borden girls." He gave a frustrated sigh and shook his head. "We need to find a common solution that will not have our wives asking questions."

"I cannot believe it has come to this. We've indulged this hobby of theirs long enough. Something must be done." This sentiment came from the head of the Shrove family, whose daughter was also suspected of being a member of Lizzie's group. There was an untouched glass of twenty-year old scotch resting in front of him.

"But what can be done?" asked Mr. Brayton under his mustache. "These women are headstrong and filled with their ridiculous delusions of suffrage and equality."

"There may be a solution that suits all of our needs, Gentlemen," Andrew stated with melancholy in his voice. Each of the men sat and listened with deep interest as Andrew explained to them his rather simple plan. An excursion that would take them out of the country and leave them under the watchful eye of a chaperone from the Church.

"Then it's settled," stated the man at the head of the table. "We'll send the girls on a grand tour of Europe. They're all the rage, and the girls will thank us later. Andrew will have his cousin Thomas make all the arrangements." The men stood and toasted their brilliant idea and congratulated themselves under an umbrella of cigar smoke.

*****

"So the European vacation was really a way to keep Lizzie and her friends safe and out of trouble?" Henry asked as he scrounged in his backpack for a snack.

"Yes," Varick replied. "The trip was intended to occupy their summer with Church activities and charity work while business relationships were mended and continued to thrive back in Fall River. There was also the added hope that maybe one of these matronly maidens, more specifically Lizzie and Emma, would be introduced to a gentleman that they might consider marrying, but as it turned out they were introduced to something much more."

*****

"What do you mean leaving? To where?" Felicity rose from her chair and started to tramp around the room while twisting her long braid in her hands.

"Yes, and for how long?" asked a voice with a nasal accent. There was a bandage covering Constance's nose, and her eyes were surrounded by dark bruises.

Lizzie was sitting on a stool in front of an upright cabinet-style piano that had a three-piece front panel elaborately decorated with scenes from the Bible. "Our father." She paused and waved her hand across a group of women sitting around the room. They were gathered in a cool, dry basement of a church lit with oil lamps. "Our fathers," she continued, "have decided to send us on a summer excursion." Murmurs spread throughout the room. Some confused and some angry.

"Now, now, ladies," Lizzie ordered, and the room fell silent. "It seems that Ellen, Anna, Carrie, Elizabeth, and Sarah along with Emma and I will be departing for a tour of Europe tomorrow. We'll be leaving at noon." She glanced down at her calloused hands for a moment. When she looked up, most of the women in the room were hanging their heads in anguish. Ellen Shrove was wiping tears from her eyes with a lace handkerchief, while Carrie and Anna Borden, distant cousins to Emma and Lizzie, consoled each other. Elizabeth and Sarah Brayton sat like stoics, showing no emotion, reminding Lizzie of the sisters' strong-willed father.

"What will happen to the group?" Deborah shrugged and adjusted the shawl covering her thin, pointy shoulders. Her voice was reserved like that of a bashful child. "What will we do?"

"First of all, you will continue to do God's work," Lizzie encouraged as she rose from her seat. "No matter what happens, we will never falter. Neither oceans apart, nor death, will not stop us from doing what needs to be done." She raised her chin and examined the girls. "Is that understood?"

"Yes," they answered in unison while eagerly nodding in agreement.

"Felicity," Lizzie instructed, "Constance and Deborah will be under your direction, and you will continue to obstruct the whorehouses and opium dens. Do not let your faith in God waver. Remind these heathens that we are not to be swept under the rug like dust." She glanced over the room, and all of the women were now standing, breaming with enthusiasm when she added, "If you have any doubts, then look to Bridget. I trust her. She will guide you in the right direction." The enthusiasm level dropped significantly as Bridget, who stood with her hands on her waist, nodded in accordance. The majority of the women objected to the housekeeper's participation in the group for various reasons, and they each had expressed their opinions with Lizzie at one time or another.

For one, they were Episcopalians, descendants of the Great Migration, while Bridget was a Catholic immigrant, from Ireland of all places. They grumbled that her Roman superstitions had no place in their group and that the community will turn against them when they find out that they're working with a Papist. However, the biggest concern was voiced by her closest companions and had to do with what they termed "the unusual relationship" between Lizzie and her housekeeper. It was their opinion that Lizzie's liberal relationship with Bridget encouraged the housekeeper to behave as if she were on an equal status with the women, completely forgetting her station in life. In addition, the group worried, and not without reason, that the one who truly had Lizzie's ear was the housekeeper. Lizzie avoided these complaints as much as possible and made it clear to the group that she considered their opinions to be the seeds of jealousy planted by the devil aimed at dividing them.

The following morning, after a light brunch, the women along with their families gathered at the harbor to say their goodbyes. Tears were shed, and slobber-filled sentiments were gargled through handkerchiefs. Constance winced when she wiped the mucus from her bruised nose while Felicity nervously chewed on the end of her long braid. The Brayton girls were being given a stern talking-to by their father, and Ellen Shrove was hugging—no, squeezing—her mother as her father was chagrined.

Andrew Borden was offering a few parting words of advice to Lizzie and Emma while Abby, their father's second wife, waited impatiently in a nearby carriage. "How much longer, dear? There's a lace fabric at McWhirr's—"

"Yes, my dear. I'll only be a moment longer," Andrew replied. "Remember, you're Bordens, so behave like it," he added before walking briskly toward the carriage. "You will have all the fabric you desire, my dear."

Lizzie and Emma watched with contempt as their father groveled to his wife and then gave each other a satirical look like children enjoying an inside joke. They picked up their matching carpetbags and started for the other women waiting to board the steamer.

"Elizabeth," a voice whispered from behind them. Both women turned and saw Bridget standing in the shadows of the dock far away from everyone else.

"I'll see you on the ship," Emma patted Lizzie on the shoulder reassuringly, and walked away.

"I didn't think you would come," Lizzie expressed as she walked to meet Bridget in the shadows. Maggie was always more comfortable in the shadows. They embraced and gave each other a kiss on the cheek. "I will miss your guidance, Maggie." Lizzie sighed, placing a palm on Bridget's cheek.

Bridget said nothing. She stepped back and reached under her dust cap and brought out a small glass cylinder filled with a translucent liquid, capped, and sealed with wax. She extended her hand and grimly ordered Lizzie to take the bottle. Lizzie took the bottle from Bridget and put it to her nose and inhaled, trying to catch a hint of an odor through the sealed wax. "What is it?"

As was her habit, Bridget offered only silence and handed Lizzie a sealed envelope. "What's with all the secrecy? I am not going to visit the Vatican, Maggie," Lizzie joked as she reached for the envelope. Bridget gave her a stern look and began to explain to Lizzie the purpose of her departing gifts.

"Our work here is very…splendid, but it is not sufficient. We are merely throwing snowflakes at a bonfire. The evil in Fall River is ancient and must be dealt with accordingly." Her Irish accent poured out like a warm stout as she spoke. She massaged a steel-beaded rosary in her hands that Lizzie had not noticed before.

"When you are in Ireland, you will go to Rosscarbery Bay and Visit St. Fachtna's monastery. Take this letter with you, and keep the bottle close at hand. You will know who to speak with when you arrive, then all of your questions will be answered." She caressed Lizzie's hands. "And you must go alone!" she stressed. "Now go. They are waiting." Bridget gestured her long chin toward the ship.

"Maggie?" Lizzie tried to speak, but Bridget herded her in the direction of the ship and withdrew to the shadows.

Lizzie held tight to the letter and bottle as she neared the boarding platform. "What did she want?" hissed one of the Brayton sisters as Lizzie passed her to board the *RMS Scythia*. Their transport across the pond.

"Only to say goodbye," she said calmly. Her eyes met with Emma's as she stepped on board, and she looked away in self-reproach. She was never good at keeping secrets from her sister.

The women lined themselves along the railing of the ship to bid a final farewell to those who remained to see them off. The only remaining family were Anna and Carrie's parents. Their mother was sobbing on her husband's lapel. Felicity, Constance, and Deborah were following the ship as it drifted apart from the dock. Lizzie spotted Bridget eyeing her from the shadows, aiming an index finger at her temple. A gesture the women used to remind themselves to focus on the task. Lizzie casually tapped her own temple and then joined the other women in waving kerchiefs at the parting continent. "Europe, here we come," she whispered to herself as she stuffed Bridget's gifts under her dress.

*****

Although the nineteen-week grand tour was intended to remove Lizzie and her friends from Fall River because of the trouble they were causing in Massachusetts, the women were anxiously anticipating all that Europe had to offer. Classic architecture and art, as well as the prospect of fine dining, as they were told this would be the focus of the trip. However, much of the tour consisted of religious excursions under the watchful eye of the meddling chaperone appointed by their Church congregation.

A chaperone was to be expected, but they had the misfortune of being accompanied by a high school teacher and church member from Taunton, who was known for being beyond reproach and chosen as the girls' chaperone for obvious reasons given the circumstances. Miss Cox was a stern woman who, it was said, could cause the strictest of Sisters at any convent to recoil in apprehension. Regardless, Lizzie had to think of a plan that would allow the women to break from their ward from time to time so they could participate in a little crusading, and so Lizzie could make good on her promise to Bridget. Until then she would do as expected of her and enjoy the tour. And that's exactly what she did.

*****

Their grand tour commenced once they crossed the pond and arrived in Liverpool. After some days in England, they made their way to the continent where they would immerse themselves in all that mainland Europe had to offer. The history, the art, the fashions, and the food.

They visited such landmarks as Belgium's the Cathedral of Our Lady, where Lizzie was in awe of the cathedral's enormity and presence. The building made the Cathedral of St. Mary of the Assumption back in Fall River seem like a boarding home in comparison. Its grand spire clocktower rivaled Big Ben, and the architecture was an amazing example of the Brabantine Gothic style. It was no wonder, as the tour guide informed her and the ladies, that the location had been chosen as the site of the diocese of the Catholic Church until 1801. Although Lizzie considered the opulence and elegance of the building as a squander and symbol of the Catholic Church's vainglorious worship of gold, she ironically appreciated the beauty that, in her opinion, could only have been created by man through the inspiration of God.

She experienced the same feelings of amazement when she was walking about and examining the many works of art on display at the cathedral and she set her eyes on Ruben's, *The Resurrection of Christ.* The Baroque masterpiece consisted of three panels. The center panel was the main attraction, with Jesus shown in all his glory donning pristine white cloth and a halo as bright as the sun. The other two panels, according to the description provided by the cathedral, were John the Baptist on the left and Martina of Rome on the right. "Catholics and their millions of saints," Lizzie said under her breath. "Saints for this, and saints for that."

The figure of St. Martina seemed lonely to Lizzie. Standing on the sidelines all by herself looking away from the commotion, holding what appeared to be a straw of wheat. Meanwhile John the Baptist, who stands alone as well, but with his gaze upon the commotion, is a participant to the resurrection. One of the boys.

Yet what truly attracted Lizzie to the painting was that Ruben had depicted Christ as a conqueror. Warrior. Victor. Not as a martyr, or as a powerless victim of a government lynching pinned to a wooden cross. She was "taken away" by the image of commoners, sinners, and soldiers cowering in fear at the feet of the Son of God, bearing his own standard, poised to move forward and fight. She thought of Felicity, Maggie, and the others and was instantly filled with pride.

The tour continued through the Netherlands and onto Germany where the women had the opportunity to explore the Royal Palace, *Dresdner Schloss*, which was beginning the renovations being conducted in honor of the House of Wettin. One of Europe's oldest houses. It was an arduous whirlwind of excitement, and they spent energy going from country to country in a nineteen-week period, attempting to see all that was worth seeing.

"Verne's Phileas and Passepartout must have had to overlook the treasures of the world in order to make their eighty-day deadline. What a shame," Lizzie pondered as she turned in each evening after a taxing day of excursions.

The women were entirely engulfed with sightseeing, souvenir shopping, and taking advantage of the opportunity to purchase the latest European boutique fashions that would not be arriving in the States until the fall. They would be the talk of the town when they returned home. Also, to the surprise of the women, their chaperone Miss Cox was not as restrictive as they had predicted. And at times was actually fun.

It was not until the group made their way to the ancient city of Rome, and Lizzie found herself surrounded by the foreboding structures and icons of the Catholic Church that she was reminded of the cylinder and the envelope. She grew solemn, and her thoughts were once again focused on devising a plan of escape from the tour, and the chaperone, so she could deliver Maggie's letter. There was also the hope that the women would be able to break away and put in a little work in the name of God. Although they were preoccupied with the tour, Lizzie could tell the women were getting restless. Especially her sister, Emma.

"Elizabeth," a voice called out, and her mind returned to the moment. "It's so beautiful. Come over here. You must have a look. We should take a photograph." It was Ellen shrove. She was waving her hand, holding a handkerchief. Her large navy-blue bonnet shaded her face from the sun, but you could still see her pleasant smile.

Lizzie approached the group. They were assembled in front of the waist-high concrete wall enclosing the Fontana Di Trevi, Rome's largest fountain. The Brayton sisters were standing a few feet apart from the others, giggling at each other. Sarah had her back to the fountain. She was shaking three Italian coins in her right hand and giving her sister Elizabeth a sheepish grin.

"Who are you going to marry, huh?" teased Elizabeth.

"Who says I want to get married? I may just toss one coin in and not all three," Sarah replied.

Miss Cox was dipping her hand into the water to test the temperature with Emma at her side, while Ellen and Carrie were warning Anna not to lean too far over the wall, or she might fall in. The water was pristine and as blue as the sky it reflected. Lizzie joined the women to admire the fountain and its grand sculpture of King Neptune commanding the oceans. Opting which horse to unleash from his chariot. The rage of the hurricane or the glassiness of a tranquil sea.

*****

It was a tranquil sea that carried them across the channel. Lizzie was leaning against the ship's railing, admiring the vast glassy desert. The tour circuit was coming to an end soon, and they would be back in England and then off to the States. There was a visit to Scotland planned and from there a quick crossing to Ireland, which happened to be Lizzie's desired destination.

"You want some company?" The question startled Lizzie, and her shoulders tightened.

Emma walked up beside her and leaned on the railing. "It sure is beautiful."

"Yeah," Lizzie replied.

"Well, are you going to tell me what Maggie has got you into that has had you so distracted all this time?" her sister inquired. Lizzie looked at Emma without answering.

"I saw you two talking before we left. I know she has you running about on some sort of secret mission," Emma continued.

Lizzie tried to remain silent, but she could feel her sister's eyes on her. That look of sympathy and understanding that always opened up Lizzie's heart and mouth.

"Darn you," she complained, and a small smile appeared on Emma's face. "I told her I would keep it between us until the time was right." She bit her lip and stared out toward the horizon.

Emma studied her sister's mood. "Alright. I trust that you'll stay out of harm's way." She turned to leave but quickly paused and added, "I'll be having a talk with our housekeeper when we get home."

Lizzie's head drooped slightly, and Emma went to her cabin.

CHAPTER 8

Revelations

Lizzie's torso swayed to and fro with each clop of the horse's hoof. It waddled its way up and down the long winding stone road that led to Rosscarbery from Clonakilty where the women happened to be staying. It was only an eight-mile ride, but her bottom was beginning to ache. She had to rent the old horse from a local farmer, which upset her because her finances were running extremely thin from the never-ending sightseeing and souvenir shopping throughout the grand tour And, she recently had to wire her father for more funds for the passage home because, for some odd reason, her family had provided her with a one-way ticket.

The night was moist, and the clouds were heavy, concealing the stars and the moon, causing the sky to appear darker than coal. Lizzie's vision only went as far as the meager glow of light from the lantern she had tied to the end of a branch allowed. Beyond that, everything was black, including the air. She held her shawl closed with one hand and held the branch with the other. She was thinking about dismounting from the old gray mare to stretch her legs, when she saw sporadic spots of faint lighting begin to expose itself.

Lampposts and fireplaces, she thought. *That must be Rosscarbery.*

She rode into the empty town like a cowboy searching for a place to wet his tongue, eyeing each silhouetted building for signs of life. She arrived at the center of town and dismounted unnoticed, or so she thought.

*****

A thin shape shrouded by the evening's darkness sat perched atop Castle Salem, keeping its swamp-green, bloodshot eyes on Lizzie. A hooded, dark-crimson cloak—almost black—draped itself around the gaunt, crouching figure and hung over the roof's edge. Its chest wheezed and gargled with each exhale of cold breath that blended with the chilled air. It continued to watch as Lizzie searched the town and the landscape.

"She seeks the church," it hissed. A long-fingered, pale, and anorexic hand with overgrown nails, more akin to claws, reached up and pulled the hood of its cloak forward to further conceal itself. After which it dropped from the building and floated to the ground.

*****

Lizzie could see no sign of the church from where she was standing in the middle of the town. No steeple. No bell tower, nothing. Her patience was running thin, her bottom hurt, and her head craved a pillow.

She guided the old gray mare down the main thoroughfare and continued to search the shadows of the landscape but could see no sign of a church. No steeple. No bell tower, nothing. The town was deserted, which seemed odd. Lizzie was hoping she could visit the town pub and inquire with the locals about the church's location, but it too was closed. She walked up and peered through the windows. The sign read *O'driscoll's*. The chairs and barstools were placed upside down on the tables and bar top, and there was a broom and mop leaning against the door on the inside.

"Damnit! What a night to be closed," Lizzie cursed to herself. She was about to head back for the cottage in Clonakilty when she decided to backtrack through the town. As she walked with the horse the clouds parted, like the Sea of Reeds did for Moses, giving Lizzie enough light to take notice of several stout figures gathered in a grassy knoll toward the placid coast of Rosscarbery Bay. Behind the figures stood a large rectangular shape. It was St. Fachtna's.

The figures were headstones in a massive graveyard. Many of them in the shape of the Celtic cross. The church stood amid the graveyard headstones in the center of a green fur-covered meadow abutting the bay. Its spire rose like an empty black mast atop a dark-gray sailing vessel buoyed in the middle of a sea of rolling dark-green swells. The headstones themselves looked like cargo that had been thrown overboard, bobbing and floating in the sea. Lizzie smirked, remembering their raid on the harbor. There was a long gravel path that crossed between the headstones and led to the church entrance at a perpendicular angle.

"Well, here we go," she whispered to the horse and patted its muzzle. She wiped horse saliva from her dress and reached under her shawl to feel for the envelope and bottle.

*****

The thin shape observed Lizzie talking with the horse before heading up the path that led to St. Fachtna's. It was concealing itself among the headstones, allowing the black night to camouflage its presence. Its dark cloak moved with the wind and fused with the surrounding atmosphere like blood mixing with red paint.

"What is her business with the church?" it pondered. "What is so significant about this one? She's no different from the others in the group, or any other tasty morsel for that matter." Wheezy bubbles moved around in its lungs as it inhaled deeply, allowing its chest to grow larger. The dark hooded cloak appeared to be shrinking as it tightened around its expanding torso while it glared at the church from under the drooping hood. "Orders must be obeyed," it hissed through its ancient, yellow-jagged teeth, and then it jumped into the air.

*****

The horse whinnied as Lizzie cautiously led the two of them up the path. She nervously glanced from side to side like a guilty child as they moved. The gravel crunched under her feet and scraped the horse's hooves with each trepid step. She left the gravel path to tie the horse to the last headstone before the church, and then she unattached her lantern from the branch before continuing to the entrance. Suspicious eyes that were keeping watch for far more sinister threats than a woman in a blue bonnet and matching shawl watched her approach with interest.

She stopped a few feet away from the portico and raised her lantern to get a better perspective of the gloomy entryway. The light revealed a set of rounded wooden doors that created an arch and were reinforced with iron slats, along with gilding that looked like some sort of dancing dragon.

Swallowing the nervous lump in her throat, she raised her hand and gave a few knocks on the heavy doors with the butt of her palm. The sound was thick and muffled. She knocked again and adjusted her shawl to warm herself. Her time was short, so she lowered the lamp and placed the flat of her hand on the left door and pushed. The door opened with a hollow groan, exposing the dimly lit space.

"Thank you, Lord," she prayed and crept inside the church, carefully closing the wooden door behind her. "Hello," she called as she stood near the vestibule. A low echo answered her back: "Hello, hello, hello." She put out her lantern and removed her bonnet, set them on a small stool, and continued into the nave.

As Lizzie walked down the aisle and between the wooden benches, she grew impressed with their polish and how pronounced their glow was in the sparsely lit area. "Hello," she called out again, and again an echo answered. She advanced toward the altar where numerous stumped, dripping candles lit the background and reflected the images on the stained-glass windows above it. There was a brighter light bleeding into the room from an area above the lectern. She hastily headed for the light while hidden eyes watched with increasing curiosity.

The light was coming from a small hallway that led to a doorway of a study and sitting room. The door to the room was wide open and Lizzie, holding her hand close to her bosom where she hid the letter and bottle, walked in disturbing a priest who appeared to be in his early thirties who was sitting at a corner desk examining an old text.

"Excuse me, si—" she caught herself in midsentence. "Father. I'm looking for..."

The priest instantly looked up with a shocked and offended look on his face. His hair and priest frock, both jet-black, gave his pale skin a translucent look.

"Who let you in?" he scolded as he rose from the desk and walked in Lizzie's direction, gesturing for her to leave.

"The church doors were open," Lizzie explained while the priest grabbed her arm and escorted her out into the lectern. "I'm looking for the abbott. I have a message for him."

The priest ignored her rantings while he looked around the candlelit church and continued to guide Lizzie by the arm. Now they were standing among the immaculate benches in the nave. "Bruce! I told him to lock the doors," he complained to the air. "Scottish imbecile. Where are you?" he grumbled.

"Yes, Father? You summoned?" a voice croaked from the direction of the confessional. Lizzie pulled her arm away from the priest, feeling insulted by the priest's ill-mannered behavior toward a lady, and shocked to find out that there had been someone in the church the entire time.

A lean man about Lizzie's height stepped out from inside the confessional. He had thinning ginger-red hair with fluffy sideburns that covered his ears and gave his hairless face a slender look. His arms were folded in front of him, and he wore a brown monk's robe that was a little high in the hem, making him look the simpleton.

"You failed to lock the cathedral doors again!" the priest berated him.

"Sorry, Father, I was giving the confessional a good cleaning," he replied with a deep Scottish accent.

"Escort this woman out, and make sure you lock the door. I'm a very busy man," the priest said, stressing his English accent as an implication of superiority.

"Wait!" I have a message for the abbott!" Lizzie pleaded to the priest's back as he walked away, disinterested.

"The abbott is away in Dublin, and he won't be returning until the end of the week," the priest explained over his shoulder. "Send her away," he reminded the monk. The monk gave Lizzie a weak smile and raised his hand, waving her toward the front doors.

Lizzie's heart burned with disappointment upon hearing the priest's announcement. "Not here. How can that be?" she whispered in sadness and exhaustion.

"Do these items belong to you, ma'am?" The question startled her. The monk was standing to the side of her, holding her lantern and blue bonnet.

"Yes," she replied as she took the items from the monk. "Thank you."

"My pleasure, ma'am," he replied as he kept escorting Lizzie out. His accent was as thick and heavy as haggis, causing Lizzie to strain her ears to understand, and his gait was slow and uneven, displaying the reason for the high hem. "I must remember to lock the doors. It can't happen again," he said aloud, in hopes that the priest was listening as he opened the wooden door.

The sound of the lock was all Lizzie needed to hear to realize that her promise to Maggie would not be fulfilled. Her head hung low while the monk continued to talk with himself and bolt the doors.

"So, me lassie! You're Birdie's girl, are ye? I've been expecting ye."

Lizzie looked up at the monk in time to see him raising his posture and stretching his joints.

"You? But Maggie said…" Lizzie's heart rate rose and popped out her throat.

"Birdie says a lot of things. Come on, let's get you someplace safe." His voice wasn't the same timid voice he used when speaking with the priest. The accent was still strong, but the tone was filled with assurance.

They walked to retrieve Lizzie's horse. When they reached the old mare, she was neighing and staring about nervously. This caught the monk's attention. Lizzie untied the horse while he kept watch, and they headed for the monk's quarters on the other end of the church property.

*****

The cloaked figure clung to the side of the church steeple with one arm and studied the girl and the monk as they untethered the horse. Its nails dug into the structure, and it gripped the limestone with its hairy feet. Its chest heaved, and it grew angry at the sight of the monk, but anger quickly turned to what could be described as joy; that is, if a decayed and soulless heart is capable of experiencing such an emotion. For now he was presented with an opportunity to eliminate an old enemy as well as complete a contract. A gleam appeared in its rotten eyes, and Its rodent-like ears twitched as it picked up on their conversation.

"They'll never reach the monastery," it hissed excitedly, causing sticky spittle to lap about its mouth and narrow chin. "Their blood shall be mine," it exclaimed to the sky above and slid off the steeple, drifting away like an old billing.

*****

The two shared the horse, so they could make better time, and the mare was handling well for her age.

"You have something for me?" the monk asked Lizzie as he sat uncomfortably behind her, trying to share the saddle.

Lizzie adjusted herself, reached under her shawl, and pulled out the envelope and the cylindrical bottle. The monk took the items from her and whistled when he saw the bottle.

"That's my Birdie. Always thinking," he said and handed the bottle back to Lizzie.

"You keep that close by, ye hear?" He tucked the envelope into his robe. "We'll see what it has to say when we get to the monastery."

Just as he finished his statement, the horse began to rear on its hind legs and thrash about wildly. The monk was immediately tossed to the ground, but Lizzie held fast and kept her buttocks attached to the saddle. The monk rose to his feet and helped Lizzie with calming the horse down. The mare settled a little, but her breathing was fierce, and she was foaming at the mouth. "It's okay, girl," Lizzie reassured her.

The horse whinnied and stared straight ahead in fear. Lizzie and the monk followed her stare. A black flowing shadow was moving toward them. Lizzie strained her eyes and saw that it was a tall man wearing a hooded cloak. The monk spanked the horse on the ass and urged it forward. "Run for the monastery and ring the bell three times!" he yelled at Lizzie as the horse ran off.

"What?"

"Ring the bell three times!" he yelled again. "And remember the bottle," he added.

He watched Lizzie speed away with a sense of dread and turned to face the shadow. It stood five feet in front of him, blocking the path to the monastery.

"Bruis," it said, letting the *ess* trail off at the end as if a snake was calling out to him. Its hands raised slowly, and it pulled its hood back, revealing its repulsive face. It had the ears of a bat, but they were on the sides of its head like a human, and it had a long jaw with a mouthful of yellow, jagged, bucked teeth like a rodent. The reddish-brown hair on its head was short and grew like a wide mohawk. There was a long scar that went from its left eyebrow to the edge of its mohawk. A previous gift from Bruis. "You've nowhere to run," it hissed.

The monk sized up the creature and performed the sign of the cross. "Okay, you ugly bastard!" he shouted. "Let's have a dance." He untied the white rope from around his waist and wrapped it around his right fist while he pulled the dull gray rosary from around his neck and kissed the cross.

The creature's lips cracked as they parted into a grotesque smile, breaking the sores around its mouth and exposing the elongated fangs surrounding its jagged, bucked teeth. "Crosses won't help you here!" it said before leaping forward with remarkable speed.

The monk remained still with his feet planted like boulders, anticipating the creature's attack. At the last moment, he sidestepped the soaring figure and swung the rosary in the air, hitting it directly on the scar above its eyebrow. The creature yelled as it landed clumsily on its feet, holding his eye in pain. It turned and glared at the monk, who was spinning the rosary around above his head. It was made of iron orbs and joined with steel links.

The creature threw back its long sleeves and gave a deafening shriek. They charged each other, and long fingers slashed at the monk's arm, forcing him to drop the rosary. A large hand gripped his face, and he felt himself being lifted in the air and pulled closer to the creature. Its mouth began to widen into a gelatinous abyss with dripping fangs as it drew the monk's head closer.

A white stone hit its face, striking it in the mouth. Once, twice. The third strike chipped his bucked teeth, and it dropped the monk to the floor. The creature wiped its mouth and glanced at the monk's hand. It wasn't a stone that struck its face; it was the rope wrapped around his hand.

They backed away from each other and looked to the sound of Lizzie's fleeing horse hooves. The monk reinforced the silver-razor-lined rope around his fist and circled the creature. It leapt at him again, but this time it dodged him using its tremendous speed and disappeared in a flash. The monk spun on his heels and spotted a blurry shadow heading after Lizzie. She was about thirty yards from the monastery, but the creature was closing in fast. She was urging the old mare along the last few yards, when she was instantly hit from behind and catapulted from the horse, landing at the foot of the door to the monastery in a painful crash.

She struggled to her feet, not knowing what happened, and searched for the doorbell. Her head was throbbing, and her vision was clouded from the pain. She pushed herself up and rested her body against the door, while searching above and around her for a bell. Her vision was still foggy, but she could see a bell-shaped blur off to the left of the door. Her hand reached up to grab the short bell and to pull, when her body was suddenly spun around and slammed onto the door. Her blurred vision cleared in time to see a monstrous figure standing in front of her with a raised clawed hand prepared to strike.

"Dear God!" she screamed as the door simultaneously opened, and Lizzie's body fell to the ground.

"What in…" the young monk standing in the doorway was about to ask when a clawed hand struck his cheek. His head twisted sideways, and the skin from his face landed in a wet mass on the open door just as his body dropped to the floor. Blood splattered across Lizzie's face and torso as she lay spread-eagled beside the young monk's body. The monster looked down at her.

"Nighty night," it gargled at her, extending its vein-covered arms in her direction. Long, dingy fingernails clicked in her face as she desperately searched her dress for a weapon, but she wasn't back home on a raid, so there was nothing. She placed her hands on her heart, ready to pray when the cylinder poked itself out from under the bloody shawl. In an act of pure instinct, she opened the bottle with swift dexterity and splashed the contents on the creature's hands and face.

"You bitch!" it screeched as it stepped backward and shook its body like a wet animal.

"It worked!" Lizzie gasped in surprise. She watched as fumes rose from the creature's skin while the smell of burnt garlic passed through her nostrils. The creature recuperated itself and charged for Lizzie. She held tight to the bottle, squeezed her eyes shut, and prayed. The creature was immediately brought to a halt by an invisible wall and fighting to move forward, kicking up gravel. Lizzie opened her eyes and jumped to her feet. There was a cord of steel rosary beads wrapped around the creature's arms and torso, and at the other end of the cord was Bruis, the monk. He was hunched and twisted over backward, attempting to drag the creature away.

Two more monks appeared at the doorway of the monastery with rosary and white rope in hand. "Bring the bucket!" Bruis directed them. A monk with a Romanesque nose on a round face darted away, and the other stepped over his brother's corpse and out from the doorway. He circled the creature while spinning his rosary like a lasso. Saliva splashed in the air as the creature snapped its long jaw toward Lizzie. Bruis was pulling with all his might, but the creature wouldn't budge. It glared back at the monk and rose to its full height. It heaved and expanded its chest, snapping the rosary, sending the steel beads flying outward. Lizzie and the monk hit the floor. The creature's eyes gleamed, and he took a long stride toward Lizzie's prone body. Its hair-covered feet planted themselves in front of her, and the long toenails scraped her fingertips.

"Get up, you fools!" a high-pitched voice ordered, and the creature reached for its throat in agony.

The round-faced monk had returned, and he was standing next to a wooden well bucket filled with water. He was holding onto a white rope that was coiled around the creature's neck with one hand and reaching out with the other. "Your ropes," he urged Bruis and the other monk. They flung their ropes at him, and he caught them with one hand and dropped them into the bucket. The creature began dragging him closer, like a disobedient dog on a leash. Pebbles kicked up in little brown clouds of dirt around planted heels as the round-faced monk fought to keep his distance from the creature. "Hurry," he pleaded to the others. Lizzie lay prostrate on the ground, watching in disbelief, as the creature grappled with the rope around its sizzling neck.

Bruis ran to the bucket and pulled out the now water-soaked ropes and tossed one to the other monk. He caught the rope in mid-air and started circling the creature again, forming a lasso with his rope. Brown bangs sweated against his forehead, and thick-furred brows diverted the salty liquid from his piercing yellow eyes, keeping his vision clear for the attack.

The creature's nails were nearing the round-faced monk's knuckles when it screeched louder than before and was yanked flat on its back. There was a rope coiled around both its fuming ankles, and the creature thrashed in pain, causing each of the monk's arms to flail about. It raised its head and howled, then gave a powerful thrust. The round-faced monk lost his grip, and the creature pulled the rope from its neck and threw it with such force, it landed in the far-off bay like a cannonball. It jumped to its feet, and its burning ankles teetered underneath, but it still managed to make a roundhouse kick swinging Bruis around and crashing his body into the monastery wall, causing the stucco to crack. Its hands burned when it grabbed the other rope and jerked it like a whip. The thick-browed monk's arms snapped, dislocating his right shoulder, and he fell to one knee, holding his arm in pain. The creature cracked its joints and stomped toward the kneeling monk. Lizzie acted quickly and ran for the bucket, splashing its contents across the creature's back. Smoke rose from its skin as it arched its back and turned, looking for the source of its pain. Lizzie stood motionless, holding the bucket in front of her. It reached for her but stumbled uncontrollably while burning skin and garlic filled the air.

In an instant, the creature spun on its heels and rushed to the forest behind the monastery. Bruis appeared at Lizzie's side, holding a hand to his bleeding forehead. "Run and tell your master, Abhartach!" he yelled at the fading shadow.

*****

Lizzie was sitting at the head of a rectangular table made from a yew tree centered in a large room in front of a blackened fireplace. She was holding a sturdy mug of warm whiskey and wearing the clothing of a scullery maid. Her clothing was stained with blood from the creature's attack, and the maid's frock was the only change of clothes the monks had on hand. Her steel nerves were shaken, and she trembled when taking a sip from the heavy mug.

Bruis and the two surviving monks were standing off to one side, engaged in a hushed and heated conversation. Lizzie strained her ears but could only catch portions of their grim discussion.

"Are you certain?" the thick-browed monk questioned Bruis.

"I am very certain, Michael," Bruis responded. "It was Bodach. Abhartach's number one. He still carries the scar I left him with."

"What is Abhartach's business with the girl?" Round Face asked in a grave tone.

"A very curious question, Benjamin," Bruis stated while holding his chin in contemplation.

Bruis approached the table and took a seat on one side while the other monks sat opposite of him. "The body has been taken care of," Benjamin said while scratching his large nose.

"Alec will be missed," Bruis solemnly replied. "He was a devout brother." All three bowed their heads and performed the sign of the cross. Lizzie looked to all three of them, wondering how they found it so easy to maintain their composure in light of the fact that a monster straight out of a dime-store horror novella just killed one of their brothers.

Bruis took a deep swig from the mug placed in front of him and looked to Lizzie after setting it down. "What is your knowledge of the minions of Ifrinn?"

The fireplace warmed Lizzie's face as she sat in silence while Bruis attempted to explain and make sense of the creature's existence. "It was a Dearg-dur," he told her as the other monks observed her with stern expressions on weary faces. "A bloodsucker. Our brotherhood has been battling their kind since before the Church arrived. They are the descendants of the Red Thirst," he went on. "Legend tells that she was a noblewoman who had been forced by an abusive father into marrying a heartless man who tortured her regularly. Whether it be with harsh words or by the switch. All the while her heart belonged to another, which enraged the cruel husband to no end. One night the husband, in a jealous-drunken fit, beat her to death and then he fed her body to the pigs. A year after the woman's disappearance, the contemptuous husband was found in his estate with his throat torn open as if he had been attacked by a wolfhound, and his body was drained of blood."

The thick-browed monk said something in Latin and gave another sign of the cross.

"There was also a swath of fabric from the noblewoman's dress clenched in his hand," Bruis added. "Legend or not, since that time the Dearg-dur have been living amongst the shadows and preying on humans undetected."

Lizzie's brain was scrambled. Up was down, and down was up. What was she hearing exactly, and what was that...monster? Monsters didn't exist. She knew that. But...that thing. It was as real as the day is long and her blood-soaked clothes, now burning in the fireplace, could attest to that.

"So what you're telling me is that was a vampire?" she asked in astonishment, eyes as wide as saucers.

"Of sorts," Benjamin calmly responded in his high-pitched voice while taking a sip from his own mug. "The Daerg-dur are a species of vampire. They are born hideous as you can see, and their purpose is to kill, not feed. Like an assassin."

"What does any of this have to do with me?" she exclaimed, thinking to herself: *Why did Bridget send me here?*

"It was Birdie's idea. According to this letter, she felt that ye were ready," Bruis told her, sliding the envelope on the table.

"Ready for what?" Lizzie exclaimed impatiently and confused.

"The war."

She stared Bruis straight in the eye at the statement without flinching. "Who is Abhartach?"

*****

Lizzie had the cart stop about a quarter of a mile up the road from the cottage, so she could walk the rest of the way and enter unnoticed. The old mare had run off during the commotion, never to return, so the monks had to rush her back to the cottage in Clonakilty before Miss Cox awoke. She was dreading breaking the news of the missing horse to the farmer.

The back door was unlocked just as she left it. She gently pushed it open, barely enough to slip in sideways, and closed it softly. Turning the lock and feeling very relieved, she turned to head for the goose-down bed to sleep for a minute before rising for the day with everyone else who slept through the night.

"Good evening, or should I say morning," a voice whispered behind her.

Lizzie jumped and covered her mouth with one hand to avoid yelling out. It was Emma, her older sister. She was sitting alone in the dark with her arms folded in front of her like an angry warden. She examined Lizzie and opened her mouth to scold her, but her tone instantly turned to concern when she got a good look at her sister in the scullery frock. "What happened to you. Where are your clothes?" she asked in urgency. "Where have you been?" she stood up and offered Lizzie the kitchen chair she was sitting on, and Lizzie sat down with a very large sigh of exhaustion and relief.

She then proceeded to tell Emma about the letter and the bottle that Bridget gave and her visit to the monastery. Emma stood and listened intently as Lizzie told her of the monster's attack and the story of the Dearg-dur. She did not mention Abhartach. When she finished the tale, she looked as if the weight of a thousand tons had been lifted from her shoulders. Emma knelt next to her and put her arm around her. There was no question that Lizzie was telling the truth. Emma knew her younger sister, and there wasn't a lying bone in her body. The question now was what to do with the information.

Lizzie rested her head on her sister's shoulder and was about to fall into a deep sleep when her head popped up quickly. "We cannot tell the others until we talk with Maggie," she told Emma, looking her straight in the eye as if expecting a promise.

"Okay. But from here on out, wherever you go I go," Emma lovingly scolded her. "Come. We both need to rest. The sun will be up soon, and we have a long day ahead of us." Emma reached her hand out to Lizzie, and the two turned in for the remainder of the night.

*****

"This part of Ms. Borden's adventure I know to be true to a point." Varick paused to interject. Henry looked up at him from his comfortable spot on the floor with an inquisitive expression.

"I was in Edinburgh on a visit to Scotland," Varick explained, "when I heard tell of a band of women from the States that were roaming about the United Kingdom touring houses of worship and causing quite a stir. It was them. I'm sure of it, now." He had a gleam of retribution that touched his eyes. "Furthermore, according to an associate, these women were suspected of setting fire to a local business owned by a well-connected Asian conglomerate."

"An opium den?" Henry muffled with a yawn while covering his mouth.

"Possibly." Varick was examining the ceiling of the building again, attempting to estimate the time. He looked to Henry, who was still lying on the floor, rubbing his eyes with the butt of his palms. "What is your timepiece reading?"

Henry leaned sideways and removed the silver pocket watch from his back pocket. He flipped the cover open with a flick of his thumb. "It's 5:38 a.m.," he said, closing the watch and giving it a small polish with the sleeve of his shirt and a little hot breath. "The sun should be peaking over the hillside right about now."

"Yes," Varick agreed. "We'll be staying here for the day as planned."

"That's the plan," Henry stated. "And then we'll fly this coup before we get into any trouble with the mysterious tenants."

Varick sat cross-legged on the floor next to Henry and finished reciting the unknown tale of Ms. Borden.

CHAPTER 9

The Courtesans

There was a knock at the door accompanied by a soft voice. "Breakfast, sir."

The Dean raised his head slowly and rubbed his eyes clear. "Who's there?" he asked. Open books covered his desk. The one he used as a headrest had a round watermark on the withered page from where his drool landed. "Damnit," he exclaimed while dabbing the moisture from the page with a handkerchief and gathering up the other books. "Breakfast, sir. Should I take it to the main hall?" the voice asked nervously.

The door opened, and a small boy of about seven years stood holding a silver serving tray. The tray wavered from the weight in the boy's hands and behind his false smile his face expressed that he was about to drop it. "No, no. Bring it here. Set it on the desk," the Dean directed the boy. He placed the tray on the desk and stepped aside to wait. The Dean was unbuttoning his shirt and sorting through a wooden wardrobe for fresh clothing, when he noticed the boy waiting silently.

"You're excused."

"But what about the dishes, sir?" the boy questioned.

"They can wait," the Dean responded. "Tell Gina to meet me in the main hall. We have plans to discuss" he ordered the boy as he slipped his arms through the long sleeves of a white button up. The boy ran out of the room, very relieved. *The Dean is in a good mood this morning*, he thought.

The Dean picked at the breakfast: oranges, fried eggs, and corn bread, and barely tasted his coffee. His thoughts were preoccupied with devising a plan. He sat at the desk and started flipping through the books again. "There has to be something here?"

Thirty minutes later, the Dean walked into the throne room, wearing his corduroy coat, and waving a hand in the air as if he were listening to a secret song. Gina and the Dean's personal attendants gave each other curious looks as he trotted to his tune and plopped down in his throne, jovially kicking one leg over the other.

He eyed Gina, focusing on the fading bruise on her cheek. "We have an amazing opportunity before us," he began with the brightest gleam in his gray eyes. "As the sham of the Piltdown Man can show, the question of human evolution and the origin of mankind is our greatest obsession." His posture straightened, and he placed his hands on the arms of his throne, gripping them in excitement.

Gina grew more confused as the Dean went on about the scientific method, nature versus nurture, and other topics that were unfamiliar to her. "What did he summon me here for?" she wondered.

"For millennia, mankind's greatest minds have postulated that humans have evolved from a few strains of primate stemming from Africa and Asia. Many a boffin have built their entire reputation and staked their entire careers on the theory of evolution based on the idea that mankind went through several logical stages of development beginning with Cro-Magnon and Neanderthal and spearheading toward Australopithecus and onto Homo sapiens."

Gina noticed the two attendees were giving their fullest attention, appearing to be enthralled with the Dean's speech, although she knew that they didn't understand half of what he was saying.

"During this pursuit," the Dean went on, "many of them have overlooked, perhaps intentionally, the possibility of the development of another species of Homo sapiens. An enhanced species.

"Since Darwin and Wallace, scientific minds have assumed human evolution progressed like a chain where each stage of development linked with one another. However, sometimes a chain splits and diverts itself like a fork in the road, producing a similar chain that evolves under different circumstances." His eyes sparkled with energy at the idea. "Therefore, resulting in a species much alike the other in appearance but quite the opposite in mindset, conduct, and subsistence."

At the mention of a fork in the road, the two boy servants nodded enthusiastically. "Yeah, like a fork," one said.

"Uh-huh," the other moronically agreed with wide-open eyes. "A fork, and a spoon." Gina flinched at their comments, waiting for the Dean to berate them for their stupidity, but fortunately for them he was too enraptured with his own voice that he failed to take notice.

The Dean stood up from the throne and folded his hands behind his back. "Yet today, in these grim times, fortune has smiled upon us and has given us the chance of a lifetime to observe and interact with what may be a living example of such a species. The next step in hominid evolution." He swept the empty room with his eyes as Gina and the two attendees were his only audience, but in his mind, he pictured a lecture hall filled to capacity with professors and PhD candidates all standing on their feet, applauding and cheering his findings.

"Summon Timothy and have him assemble the bravest children in the main corridor under the reception building. Tell them to arm themselves as well. We are about to engage on a mission that will bear great consequences in the name of science."

*****

Elizabeth and her entourage were away in Europe for nineteen weeks and returned to the States in late November. Winter was around the corner. The weather was piercing, and the leaves on the trees were no longer green.

The ship docked without incident as the women huddled near the railing and stood by for the landing plank to drop. A crowd was assembled on the pier to greet the returning voyagers. Business associates, lovers, wives, and coachmen were all there to receive their counterparts. Among them were family members or household domestic workers who were waiting patiently in the cold to transport the women home. The women embraced and said their goodbyes before parting, while their luggage was loaded onto their transports.

Lizzie and Emma sat in silence across from their father, Andrew, and his wife, Abby. They weren't expecting their stepmother Abby to be there as they were hoping to speak with their father alone about the trip.

"Why the long faces?" their father asked eyeing them both. Abby was snuzzling in her fur cloak, trying to keep warm and ignoring the girls at the same time.

"The trip was exhausting," Emma responded. Lizzie remained silent as she stared out the carriage window, recalling the conversation she had with the women before leaving the ship. She didn't tell them about her excursion at the church, but she did stress that they had something very urgent to discuss. They agreed to meet in two days in the church basement, giving them enough time to catch up with their loved ones and unwind from the trip.

Nothing else was said throughout the journey until they arrived home where Bridget was there to greet them with a grand smile and a home-cooked meal. The expertly prepared meals and exquisite pastry shops of Europe were a terrific experience, but nothing could satisfy Lizzie and Emma's taste buds like Maggie's clam chowder, along with crab cakes and Boston brown bread.

After unpacking and feasting on several pieces of brown bread, Lizzie and Emma shared the details of their trip with their father and Abby. They sat in the warm dining area and recounted their visiting the fountains of Rome and streets of France. Abby's interest grew when they talked of Paris and its plethora of jewelers and vogue boutiques. Their father paid special attention as they described the fortresses and castles of England and Germany. Emma was discussing the many cathedrals of the Netherlands, when Bridget began to clear the table of dishes. Lizzie took the cue and stretched her arms wide over her head and yawned loudly. She kicked Emma's shin under the table and caused her to jump in surprise. She quickly recovered and began to rub her eyes, giving a convincing yawn as well.

"Off to bed, you two," their father exclaimed. "You can share more about your trip tomorrow."

Abby rose to her feet. "Your father is right." She patted Emma on the shoulder and left the dining area. The fireplace kicked sparks as she walked past. Andrew wiped his hands and brushed the crumbs from his lapels with his napkin and left his seat to follow her out. "Good night, girls."

*****

"Bridget," Lizzie whispered. She and Emma were standing near a crumbling stone wall at the edge of a vacant farm. They were concealed under black riding cloaks and standing very close together, trying to keep warm.

"Why couldn't we just meet at the house where we live?" Emma complained sarcastically from under her hood. "If you can recall, we were already there." She pulled her cloak closer to her.

"Bridget insisted," Lizzie replied. "Bridget," she whispered again.

"Over here," an Irish accent called out from the direction of a gnarled, leafless black tree that was a hundred years dead.

The two sisters climbed over the crumbling wall and headed to the tree. Bridget stepped out from behind and stopped short when she saw Emma. "I told you to come alone."

Lizzie looked at Emma. "She knows everything already."

"Yeah. And from now on, wherever she goes, I go," Emma added, moving closer to Lizzie.

"Nothing can be easy with you two girls." Bridget sighed.

Emma and Lizzie lowered their hoods, exposing proud grins, and the three took a seat on the dead tree's vast roots that popped out of the ground like swollen knuckles on an arthritic hand.

"I met with your friends," Lizzie said flatly, unflinchingly staring at Bridget. "You should have warned me, Maggie."

"Would you have believed me?" she asked sympathetically.

"I suppose not," Lizzie respectfully replied as she looked down at her lap and smoothed her cloak.

"I wanted you to know exactly what we're up against," Bridget explained.

"But I nearly lost my life," Lizzie complained before going into the details of the attack at the monastery. Bridget sat and listened unaffected by the gory details of Lizzie's first encounter with an immortal. When she finally finished her story, Bridget leaned forward and put a hand on Lizzie's knee. "Now you're ready to lead us" was all she said.

The two days passed faster than an hour, and the women found themselves sitting in the church basement trading stories and catching up on all the latest gossip. Ellen was pretending to hold a cigarette in her hand and walking with an exaggerated step in imitation of a high-society woman in front of Constance and Felicity, who were sitting on a wooden bench giggling at one another. Deborah was sitting across from the Brayton sisters, sharing something very interesting judging from the intense look on the girls' faces, and Carrie and Anna were walking around the basement handing out some of the confectionary treats they brought back from Europe.

Lizzie sat in front of the piano, watching the women behave like adolescents in a social club, knowing that after tonight what was left of their naivety would be washed away like original sin cleansed through baptism. Emma was sharing the piano bench with Lizzie, while Bridget sat on a large wooden crate in the corner of the basement darkened by the shadows as usual.

Lizzie allowed the women to frolic for a few more minutes before lifting the piano's keyboard cover and slapping her palm on a random group of keys. Everyone straightened their postures in attention at the sound of the unstructured notes, and those standing scattered to find a seat. Lizzie stood and paced leisurely around the room like a smitten schoolgirl taking a stroll in a field of flowers.

"It's so nice having all of us together again," she stated as she passed Constance and lovingly patted her on the head. Her nose had healed since the raid on the dock, but there was a slight curve to it now. "The trip to Europe was dreadfully long, but my thoughts were constantly on returning home to pick up where we left off."

A joyful rumble filled the basement. Lizzie smiled at the women, causing her gray eyes to glimmer, and she continued. "Now, I know that those of you who had the great fortune to remain here in Fall River while the rest of us were away have been successfully working to maintain the order we have brought to this city. On my way here, I noticed that the Sixth Street brothel has been boarded up." She looked at Felicity and tilted her head in congratulations. A tiny smile touched the corner of her mouth, and she proudly nodded in recognition of Lizzie's praise.

Lizzie halted her pacing among the women in the center of the room and turned slowly, giving the women a stern look. The jovial mood disappeared from the room, and the climate became serious as she began to speak.

"The battles we have been engaging in thus far have borne fruit by revealing to the people of Massachusetts the sin that exists in plain sight in their community backed by those in power who profit from vice." She spoke with an urgent resolve that alarmed the women. This was not the Lizzie they were familiar with. This person sounded more like a returning soldier who had witnessed the gruesome tragedies of war firsthand.

"Yet throughout all our efforts, we have only been able to scratch the surface of the devil's playground and have failed to confront the real enemies of Christ." The women grumbled their consternation and looked at one another in confusion as Lizzie walked back toward the piano and stood beside a grave-looking Emma.

"However, do not take this to heart. It is not because of laziness or lack of effort on our part why we have failed, but by the machinations and illusions that are put into play by powerful, age-old entities who lay hidden in the background, pulling the strings of society's most influential members."

The women practically fell over the edge of their seats listening to Lizzie tell her tale of the creature's savage attack and the group of vampire-hunting monks. The Borden sisters, Emma and Lizzie's cousins, were fearfully clenching their hands together like knots, and Constance was huddled closely with Deborah as Lizzie described the creature and how its skin burned from the garlic water. She then went on and told them the story of the Daerg-dur as well as the knowledge that Bruis had shared with her about vampires.

When she finally finished her recounting, she was back near the piano, and Emma was standing at her side. There was no immediate reaction from anyone, and then the room stirred with activity and hushed murmurs. Some of the women stood and stared at Lizzie in disbelief, while others remained seated and gave each other skeptical glances as if they were questioning her sanity. Felicity was pacing anxiously in a corner, wringing her long braid and talking to herself the way she does when she's nervous, or scared. Bridget was calmly stooping over, picking up something from beside the crate.

"Vampires," the Brayton sisters said in unison.

Felicity quit her pacing and addressed Lizzie. "This is all because of her," she said, pointing an accusing finger at Bridget. "Her and her Catholic superstitions. She should have never been able to—"

"Get ahold of yourself, woman," Emma interrupted, giving felicity a stern look. She shut her mouth in midsentence and grabbed her braid again and continued her pacing.

"I believe you, Lizzie," Ellen said sympathetically. "But what does that have to do with us? I mean, what are we to do?"

Lizzie and Emma glanced at one another and walked forward. The women parted the room for them as they headed for the rear of the room, where Bridget was now standing next to the crate with an iron crowbar.

The women gathered around the crate, while Bridget tore into it with the crowbar and lifted the lid. The nails pulled away with a dry screech, like an unoiled hinge. Lizzie and Emma grabbed the lid and lifted it off the crate as Deborah jumped in to help. They set it against the wall below the small basement window. The crate was filled with wood shavings to the brim. Lizzie reached in and rummaged around under the wood shavings, until she found what she was searching for. She pulled her arm from under the shavings, causing a few to fall onto the floor and held out a bundle of small arrows with a single groove along the shaft.

They emptied the contents of the crate onto a rectangular table in the center of the basement, and they stood surrounding it, admiring the display. The table was covered with a pile of bundled yew arrows tipped with silver and a row of crossbows that held six arrows at a time. There was also a stack of white ropes woven with silver blades lined up next to a dozen or so rosaries made of steel with beads as large as cherries. The women eyed the rosaries suspiciously. Lizzie grabbed one of the of the ropes and whipped it at the piano bench, wrapping it around one of its legs, and pulled. The leg tore away with ease, and the bench leaned over, hitting the floor.

"That is what we are going to do."

*****

"Thus, the company of courtesans was born," Varick stated.

"The what company?" Henry lifted his head to ask.

"If you can recall some days ago, when you began nagging me to tell you the tale of Ms. Borden, when I first mentioned a *Company of Courtesans."* Varick was staring at Henry impatiently, waiting for an answer as dawn was opening to a bright sunny day, and he was looking forward to resting before they made their departure from the mysteriously eerie minigolf course. Henry gave a gaping yawn that ended in a howl and nodded yes with tight, sleepy eyes.

"Well, this new-and-improved group reengaged in the usual activities of harassing whorehouses and taverns, but they eased up on the forceful tactics as to give the impression that they learned their lesson. And to give them an opportunity to observe the comings and goings of individuals they believed could lead them to their true targets.

"One particular evening, while Lizzie, Emma, and Constance were handing out church pamphlets and saving souls in front of a tavern located across from a Royal Stores, Constance espied a familiar figure walking among the throng of nightcrawlers. It was the tall, thick-necked man who was there the night of the raid at the docks. She touched her crooked nose, and her eyes tightened in anger as she watched the man enter the Royal Stores."

She turned and ran to Lizzie and Emma, who were under a lamppost speaking with a drunken merchant marine, who had everything else on his mind other than salvation. Emma was casually redirecting his wandering hands, when Constance approached.

"Guess who I just saw walking into the Royal Stores across the street?" she taunted.

Emma pushed the drunken sailor aside with ease, and he fell against the lamppost, and he slid to the floor, mumbling to himself.

"Who?" Lizzie and Emma blurted.

"The tall muscular one who you were playing footsies with on the docks." Her comment was directed at Lizzie, and her eyes brightened at the report.

"Are you sure?" her response was urgent.

Constance nodded in confirmation, and Lizzie rushed toward the Royal Stores. Emma grabbed her by the arm and pulled her to the side of the tavern, where the shadows concealed them from the streetlights.

"Patience, sister," she calmed Lizzie. "Let's wait and see where he goes," she advised.

Lizzie impatiently pulled her arm away from Emma's grip and respectfully nodded in agreement. They continued to pass out pamphlets until No Neck finally emerged from the Royal Stores. He stood in the doorway and looked left to right, taking recognizance of the area before moving. He pulled up the collar to his long black duster and headed down the street like a man with a purpose.

The three followed him to the outskirts of the downtown area, all the way to Quarry Street where he disappeared into the Barnard Mills Building near the Quequechan River. The women ran across the road and sat on a bench along the river. The streetlamp near the bench was broken, allowing the women to sit in darkness without being spotted. Two hours passed before No Neck showed his face again. He waited in the doorway and surveyed the street for several minutes, until a maroon coach pulled up in front of the building. Moments later, Silver Chops exited the doorway and boarded the carriage followed by No Neck. At the sight of Silver Chops, Lizzie and her companions gave each other cynical looks.

"I know those sideburns," Lizzie grunted.

"Isn't that the bank president?" Emma whispered.

"Not sure," Lizzie replied. "But I've seen him before. He's someone important."

The three women hurried back toward the downtown area, searching for the maroon carriage carrying the two men. It was parked outside of a local whorehouse with only the coachman on board. That meant Silver Chops and No Neck were inside partaking in sin.

"We need to get in there," Constance said, thinking of nothing but revenge for her broken nose. It was one of No Neck's cohorts who smashed her in the face that night at the docks, and she wanted nothing more than to return the favor.

"The bouncers know what we look like, so the front door is out of the question," Emma added.

Lizzie didn't hear them as she was busy examining the buildings around the brothel. There was a one-story curio shop that was part of the same structure. Above it was an open window with a purple curtain on the second story of the brothel. "Follow me," she suddenly said and ran to the back of the building. A startled Constance and Emma quickly ran after her.

"The tall one is cute" a squeaky female voice declared.

"Yeah, but he ain't the one with the money. That's why he's standing outside" a raspy voice responded. "We just gotta keep the other two happy, and our pocketbooks will be bursting by sunrise."

"I don't know," the squeaky voice trembled. "The old man is... so old, and the other one? Well, I don't like the looks of him."

"Look here. You're new at this. I get it," Raspy voice scolded. "But this ain't the time for being lily-livered. Just do as you're told, and you'll be fine. The last thing you want is the missus to get a hold of you."

There was a moment of silence before the raspy voice spoke again. "Look. I'll take the creepy one, and you can have the old man. He'll probably fall asleep snoring before you get your clothes off anyways."

There was no response, and a few moments later a door could be heard closing shut. Lizzie, Constance, and Emma were squatting beneath the window, eavesdropping on the entire conversation.

"Did you hear that?" Lizzie anxiously asked the other two. They nodded but said nothing. "They're here, and they have a friend with them." Her eyes glittered with excitement.

Emma and Lizzie cupped their hands, and Constance placed her feet inside, using them like stirrups. They lifted her until she was eye level with the small window. The purple curtain brushed her in the face when the breeze moved. She was looking into a combination changing room and latrine with wooden partitions that offered limited privacy. *Must be where the whores freshen up*, she thought. "It's empty," she reported. They lifted her higher, and she raised a leg and climbed inside.

They clung together behind one of the wooden partitions, out of sight from the door in case someone else entered the room. There were various clothing items hanging about the partition. But nothing a self-respecting Christian woman would wear. It was well past midnight, which meant that the crowd at the whorehouse was light. This would work in favor of the ladies as they were playing it by ear and acting on the spur of the moment.

"The whores in the bathroom said that the tall one was waiting outside. That must be our friend," Lizzie explained. "We have to lure him away from the room."

"I'll do it," Constance immediately volunteered. She patted her hand on the white rope around her cloak, thinking of what she was going to do when she got him alone.

*****

No Neck was standing watch outside of a room at the end of the hall near the staircase. His black duster was hanging at the head of the staircase, with two other cloaks. He yawned and leaned against the wall, thinking about filling his belly. He'd been standing guard for over two hours, making sure no one interrupted Mr. Cross's monthly meeting with his strange, pale-faced friend. Barret always took him for a foreigner; the quiet man with slicked-back white hair and the face of a twenty-five-year-old always made him feel uncomfortable, and it took a lot to make him feel uncomfortable. He had caught the man staring at him several times as if his dinner had arrived, and since then he made sure never to get within arm's distance of the foreigner.

Barret understood that the man was important, but what he never understood was why these meetings always had to take place at night. "How much longer are they going to be?" he pondered. He was well aware that their official business was finished forty-five minutes ago when the two whores arrived. Ever since then, there had been nothing but moans and groans with a little pounding here and there.

His eyes drooped, and his head sagged over his thick neck, when a figure approached from the direction of the changing room. He looked up and cleared his vision. It was another whore making her way to one of the rooms, which puzzled him because he was under the impression that the floor had been cleared for Mr. Cross and his associate, as usual. Her face was surrounded by strawberry-blond hair and concealed with a black lace mask. She wore a matching lace dress as tight as a snake's skin, revealing her most intimate areas with very high heels that had buckles in the design of red roses. She also wore a white belt woven around her waist that looked out of place. His eyes widened the closer she got. *I guess this place isn't so bad*, he thought and gave a low whistle.

She stopped in front of him, batted her eyelashes, and asked for directions as if they were meeting at a train station. Barret straightened up and smiled from ear to ear. "You sound lost, ma'am."

"Maybe," she teased and continued to walk, knowing his eyes would stick to her like glue. She headed to a room across the hall, hoping that the door was unlocked and the that it wasn't in use. It opened with ease, and the happy couple entered and shut the door behind them.

*****

Lizzie was watching the whole display through the keyhole of the changing-room door. Constance enticed No Neck and led him to one of the rooms like a carrot on a stick. *It wasn't that difficult, given her well-curved body*. Lizzie blushed at the thought.

"Okay, let's move," Lizzie ordered, and she and Emma stepped lightly along the hallway while pulling out weapons from under their cloaks, until they were in front of the door that No Neck was formerly guarding. Lizzie tested the doorknob, and it was unlocked. She pushed the door ajar, and the odor of lust and the iron stench of blood crept out of the room. The smell of blood alarmed Lizzie and Emma, so they acted fast and slammed the door open and jumped into the room armed with crossbows.

The scene they encountered was straight out of Dante. Silver chops was lounging in a large leather chair drinking a glass of liquor. He wore nothing other than silk socks and his wrinkled, naked body covered the chair like a furry blanket. There was a white-haired man sitting naked in the center of a king-sized bed caressing his paramour, but there was blood squirting from her neck and there was another, younger woman lying spread-eagled next to them with the graying skin of someone who recently died. Her throat was ripped open and blood spread across the bed giving the illusion of red silk sheets.

At the sound of their entrance, Silver Chops spit out his liquor and dropped his glass to the floor while searching for something to cover his lumpy body. The man on the bed dropped the woman, stretched his head forward, and let out a screech like a wildcat. His youthful face was covered in blood that dripped from large fangs protruding from his long, gaping mouth.

The sisters let loose and fired their crossbows until the arrows were spent. Five arrows pierced the wall, but the others landed true and pinned the white-haired man against the wooden headboard of the bed. His skin started to sizzle as the liquid garlic made its way down the grooved shaft of the arrows and into his body. His hands reached for the arrows, desperately trying to pull them out, when four more arrows were fired in his direction, yanking his arms back and pinning them to the headboard as well. The screeches grew louder, but they weren't coming from the donkey pinned to the headboard. He remained silent, tolerating the pain of his sizzling skin, while keeping a furious eye on Lizzie's every move.

The sound was coming from the direction of the leather chair. Silver Chops was crouching behind the chair in the fetal position, screaming like a baby. "Take care of that." Lizzie pointed to the chair.

Emma ran to the wrinkled ball of fur and hit him on the head with her crossbow several times until he was unconscious, splitting his skin open in the process. She kicked the door to the room closed and returned to lizzie. They stood at the edge of the bed, observing the thing pinned to the headboard for a moment, and slowly untied the white ropes that held their cloaks together.

*****

As soon as the door shut Constance turned around, pushed No Neck against the wall, and began unbuttoning his shirt. Barret grabbed her by the shoulders and held her at arm's distance to get a good look at her. Her transparent dress was causing most of the blood in is body to be diverted to his dick, making it harder than a diamond. "She'll be getting a rock-hard jewel with that pearl necklace tonight." He imagined while examining the smooth skin around her neck and shoulders.

"Take it easy, my dear," he soothed her, but she was raging with lust, and she spun him around and pushed him onto the bed where he landed on his back. She jumped on top of him and restrained his hands with hers, while she gyrated her pelvis against his. She released his hands and seductively undid the belt around her waist. She gently placed the rope around his neck and ran her fingers through the hair on his chest.

"This is my lucky night." Barrett exhaled passionately as he relaxed his body.

"Yes, it is, my dear," Constance whispered to him as she pulled away the lace mask and whipped her hair about. "Mine too."

He put his hands on the side of her face and was about to comment on her beauty, when a memory flashed through his mind, and his eyes squinted in anger. "The shipment…" was all he had time to say. The rope around his neck tightened like a noose, allowing the silver razors to cut into his flesh. His eyes bulged, and his hands frantically pulled at the rope, cutting open his fingers and knuckles. He tossed and turned on the bed, gasping for breath, pushing Constance off him, and landed on his stomach. She pulled harder on the rope, and the skin around his neck started to shred, revealing tendons and muscle. He pushed himself up on all fours and jerked his body, trying to throw her off his back, but she gripped her legs tightly around his torso, cutting off his airflow even further and rode him like a bucking bronco.

The bedposts banged against the wall in a steady rhythm. *Bang! Bang! Bang!* Downstairs the missus was counting the night's take when ceiling dust landed on the money laid out on the desk in front of her. Her eyes rolled under the heavy layers of mascara. "Sounds like Mr. Cross and his friend are having fun tonight," she smirked.

Barrett's efforts slowed, and eventually he lay lifeless on blood-stained sheets. Constance was standing next to the bed, admiring her handiwork. She touched the crooked bump on her nose, smiled, and left returning to the changing room to clean up.

*****

Lizzie and Emma turned quick at the sound of the light knock at the door. "Who is it?" Emma said in a most polite voice.

"Constance," a whisper responded.

Emma opened the door enough for Constance to slide through. She stopped in her tracks when she saw the white-haired man crucified to the headboard. Mr. Cross was sitting in a big leather chair, sweating profusely. Blood trickled down the side of his face and seeped into the fold of his neck, turning his white porkchops pink. He was dressed now, and the sweat stains around his armpits were growing larger.

"How did it go with our other friend?" Lizzie asked while tightening the restraints around Mr. White Hair's wrists. He continued to remain silent. His breathing was steady but growing thicker with the fluids filling his lungs.

"He died with a smile on his face," Constance stated flatly. Mr. Cross looked up at her in shock, realizing they were talking about his faithful assistant.

"Where is Barrett?" What did you do with him?" he demanded.

Constance walked over and patted him on the head reassuringly. "Now, now. He's better off dead, that one." Mr. Cross shivered, and a wet spot appeared on the crotch of his pants.

Lizzie hopped on the bed and stood over Mr. White Hair, twirling a single arrow in her hands. "We know what you are. The question is, who are you, Mr. White Hair?" she questioned, while planting a knee on his leg. They were face-to-face now.

He exhaled slowly. "Ms. Borden," he said as calmly as someone preparing to meditate regardless of his sizzling wounds. "I thought you would have taken the hint after Ireland."

An expression of shock briefly appeared on her face, and Mr. White Hair smiled and licked blood from his fangs. She gripped the arrow and shoved it into his collarbone. He hissed and his fangs snapped at her wrist, but she pulled away, holding the arrow before he could catch her.

"Who are you?" she demanded.

"You don't know who you're dealing with! He's a very powerful man!" Mr. Cross protested. Constance backhanded him in the face, and his fat cheek shook like a chicken's ass. He raised his hands in defense and cringed in the chair.

"He's no man." Emma was glaring at Mr. White Hair, holding a meat cleaver in her hand. Her temper was flaring as she thought of the creature that tried to kill her sister in Ireland.

Mr. White Hair said nothing and taunted her with his bright yellow eyes. "Time is short. We have to move on." Lizzie pulled a small mallet from inside her cloak and raised the arrow to his chest.

"Childish woman," he hissed and then instantly pulled his torso away from the headboard, leaving the arrows in place. He reached for Lizzie, but she held fast and lifted the hammer and arrow, aiming for his heart. Something bounced off her shoulder, and his body lurched forward, allowing the arrow to slide into his chest from the pressure. She looked down to see what hit her, and Mr. White Hair's head was resting in his lap. His bright yellow eyes and young face were petrified in surprise. Emma winked at Lizzie as she wiped her meat cleaver on the bedsheets.

The three women turned and focused their attention on the sweaty, pissed-soaked whimpering figure in the chair. "Don't kill me," he cried. "Please! I can give you money. Lots of it!" He looked around the room in desperation and kneeled in front of the women spreading his hands. "I can take care of this. I can make it disappear," he pleaded.

The women glanced at one another on the verge of giggling. "Yes, you will take care of this." Lizzie said in answer to his plea. "You will have your people take care of the bodies as is your custom," she explained while looking over at the mess on the bed. The two whores were piled on one another, and Mr. White's headless torso rested on an ass cheek.

She leaned in close to him. "But first, you will tell us everything you know about that thing on the bed and his business associates."

Mr. Cross sat in the leather chair with his head in his hands and told the story of Adrianus Coen, a Dutchman who resided in England during the reign of King James I. He claimed to have landed with his brother on what he referred to as Patuxet with the Pilgrims of the *Mayflower*. They fled England during the Calvinist persecution of the early sixteen hundreds and returned to Holland where many displaced Christian communities headed because of the region's visionary ideals of religious freedom. However, Mr. Coen never suggested that he and his brother were part of any religious community. He had stated that they were in Holland, mainly because they were suspected of being one of the conspirators of something he called the Gunpowder Plot of 1605 aimed at assassinating the king. They landed in the Americas and began investing in natural resources and became pioneers of the tobacco trade. Since then, they made sure to keep the leaders of the New World in their pockets through commercial partnerships accompanied with extortion and the constant threat of death.

He paused for a second, giving Constance a chance to ask an obvious question. "That baby face over there"—she had her hands planted on her hips and nodded toward the bed—"was close to three hundred years old?"

“Much older,” Mr. Cross groaned and then went on to explain how Mr. Coen and his sibling weren’t the only ones of their kind in very high places. They were all over the country. All over the world for all he knew, and they had their hands in everything.

When he finished his account, he pulled a moist handkerchief from his jacket and wiped the sweat from his upper lip and nose. he looked up at the women who watched him, saying nothing.

“What now?” he whined.

“You’ll do as you’re told,” Lizzie answered, while the three women gathered the arrows from the wall and headboard. They exited the room, leaving behind a whimpering Mr. Cross.

CHAPTER 10

Murder Was the Case

Bodies began turning up all throughout Fall River. Some had wooden stakes protruding from their chests, while others were beheaded or burnt to a crisp from basking in the sun. The victims were people of status: politicians, lobbyists, financiers, and industrialists, the elite of Fall River. Yet not all were vampires. Some were power-hungry mortals who had pledged their loyalties to the vampire community with the intentions that one day they would be accepted into the cabal.

The press did what they were told and suppressed the details, while the police reported the murders as the work of a serial killer, but the bodies kept showing up everywhere. A group of churchgoers discovered one tied to a lamppost on a bright Sunday morning, another was found in an upscale neighborhood on Linden Street, and one was propped up in the doorway of a bank on Bedford Street concealed from the sun with its teeth pulled.

Meanwhile, the residents of Fall River lived in fear of becoming the next fatality as several fantastic rumors spread through the suburbs, ghettoes, and farmlands. Some alleged that the killings were the result of rabid wild-animal attacks possibly done by a boar, a bear, or a bobcat. Others blamed it on Bolshevik immigrants who were exacting their revenge on the greedy capitalists. Yet the most widespread rumor was that the murders were being committed as part of a bigger conspiracy to cover up the secret machinations of the government and their tycoon bedfellows.

It was this last speculation that intrigued the power brokers all over Massachusetts. The reason being was that this particular piece of scuttlebutt was somewhat close to the truth, and they didn't need any more busybody reporters following up on the story. Moreover, it was believed that the reverberations of the killings were catching the attention of the elite all along the Eastern Seaboard, creating great concern. They had given the Fall River chapter the responsibility to handle the problem locally, but all they did was send the girls on a vacation. Therefore, grave measures had to be taken.

*****

It was a hot and muggy morning on August 4 in Fall River just as the *Post* reported. The sidewalks and streets were abustle with the usual activities. There were Portuguese boys selling their mothers' baked goods along the main avenue that was overflowing with horse and carriage traffic. Peddlers, shopkeepers, and customers ignored the smell of manure and raw sewage and went about their day. Faces smiled, and children frolicked while young lovers sneaked glances at each other, and the recent slew of mysterious killings was the last thing on anyone's mind.

Nevertheless, at midday, this peaceful monotony was shattered by the sound of dozens of "newsies" spread throughout the region, wailing the latest headline of the afternoon edition of the *Fall River Post.* "Double Homicide in Fall River: Bordens Brutally Hacked to Death, Lizzie Borden at Home During Murders." The gruesome story of the Borden murders rolled out and swept through the area like a tidal wave, forcing foamy whitewashed details into the ears of neighbors, business associates, employees, and family members.

The Bordens were a notorious family who were associated with the founding of Fall River. Their deaths were felt far and wide, and the entire community was taken aback by the ferocity of the murders, sending ripples of fear into every nook and cranny. These were unlike the other various bodies being disposed of by Lizzie and her courtesans in the still of the night. These were churchgoing, upstanding protestants, and the sheer notion that the head of a prominent family could be murdered along with his wife in the light of day just a stone's throw from the hustle and bustle of the business district was very disturbing. Furthermore, no one could come to terms with the reality that someone from their social and religious circle could commit such an act.

*****

The corpses were first discovered by Lizzie herself when she arrived home from a morning excursion. The curtains were drawn, and the shutters were closed, preventing any outside light from shining through. Her father's upper body was collapsed at an angle on the couch, and his legs slid off the side like a slouching teenager. His eye was slashed wide open, and the wounds were fresh. Yet there was hardly any blood around the body and couch, which seemed peculiar Lizzie thought.

She took a step back and observed the room for signs of entry and called out to Bridget, "Maggie, come quick."

The housekeeper entered the sitting room accompanied by the neighbor, Mrs. Churchill, who happened by. Bridget reached for the steel rosary around her neck when she spotted Mr. Borden's body. "Are you alright, Lizzie?" she asked as she roamed about the room pulling back curtains and looking out the window with the rosary wrapped around her fist.

Lizzie turned on her heels. "Abby! Where's Abby?" She ordered Bridget to check the upper floors of the house. Bridgett acted fast and darted up the stairs, with Mrs. Churchill right behind her. Before she reached the second level, she spotted Abby Borden's body on the floor of a guest bedroom.

Lizzie wiped tears from her eyes as she and Bridget stepped gingerly around Abby's body and examined the guest room. Mrs. Churchill was holding a handkerchief to her mouth, trying to control herself. Lizzie patted her on the shoulder. "Go home." The neighbor stepped quickly down the stairs, slamming the front door on her way out.

"Do you notice anything strange here?" Lizzie asked Bridget in between sniffles.

"You mean the curtains and the shutters? I opened every one of them myself this morning," Bridget swore. "Whoever was here preferred the dark."

Lizzie gestured toward Abby's body. "Anything else?"

"No blood," the housekeeper stated grimly.

"Yes. It's the same with my father." There are no signs of a break-in either."

Bridget nodded in agreement. "What are we going to do?"

"Call the police." Lizzie sniffled.

Bridgett ran to the telephone, and a sturdy knock pounded on the door as she reached for the earpiece. "Police. Open the door. We received reports of an altercation." Bridgett pulled her hand away from the telephone and glanced at Lizzie, who was giving her a concerned look.

*****

Bright flashes from photographers' folding cameras blinded Lizzie and Bridget as reporters, policemen, and Mayor John Coughlin swarmed throughout the house. The captain and another officer who seemed to be of high rank watched over them as Bridget consoled Lizzie in the kitchen, while other policemen chatted about the area and made a half-assed effort at searching the premises. They overheard a policeman explain to a reporter that the officer was George Seaver, a State Police detective who had been brought in to assist with the investigation. He had a no-nonsense face, and none of the other men dared approach him.

The two women eyed the other officers, hoping they would see a familiar face, but Lizzie and Bridget didn't recognize any of them other than the captain. The others looked foreign and out of place. They weren't Fall River boys.

They sat patiently as the officers went on socializing. The state detective was no longer in the room. The captain kept checking the time on his watch and looking directly at the staircase that led to the basement. He noticed Bridget watching him, and he nervously put his watch back in his shirt pocket and dabbed at his smooth forehead with a cloth. The hot and muggy weather was adding to the body heat and turning the kitchen into a sauna.

A moment later, a shout came from the basement. "We have something down here." The captain moved nonchalantly to the stairs and headed for the basement. He glimpsed over at Bridget and saw that she was keeping an eye on him.

"They are all in on it. Trust no one," she whispered to Lizzie as she comforted her.

Within seconds, he ascended the stairs with the detective following close behind. He was holding a tin bucket that swung in rhythm with each step he took, and the detective cradled a bulky brown paper like a baby that needed a diaper change. The captain placed the bucket on the table in front them, while the detective laid out the paper exposing several well-sharpened hatchets and two axes. There was dried blood on the handles from previous raids on vampires and their cronies. The woman peeked over the lip of the bucket and saw that it was filled with bloody rags. Lizzie wiped her nose and shoved her head into Bridget's shoulder, sobbing uncontrollably.

"Where's my sister! Get out of my way!" a voice demanded, and officers moved about until Emma emerged from a group of policemen and reporters blocking the kitchen entry. She rushed to her sister, and they embraced. After which she pulled up a chair next to Lizzie and sat to one side of her, with Bridget on the other.

The captain and the detective approached the three sitting women and focused their attention on Lizzie. The mayor stood observing as Detective Seaver questioned her about the bucket of rags and the hatchets, but she continued to sob, holding her sister, who was crying as well at the loss of their father.

When she finally gathered her senses, she explained to the men that the bloodied rags were the result of an unfortunate incident related to a woman's time of the month. "I'm sorry. I didn't have time to dispose of them properly. I'm so embarrassed."

"Now, now. It's not your fault, girl" Bridget assured Lizzie, while wrapping an arm around her. Emma and Lizzie were still holding each other, lost in their grief.

"Do we have to do this now?" Emma urged to the sergeant. "Our father was just murdered!"

The captain awkwardly shuffled his feet and wiped at the sweat at his neck as the detective and the mayor turned away and slowly headed for the door. "I'm sorry, Miss Borden. I suppose we can come back tomorrow," he said sympathetically and looked around to the other officers, hinting that it was time to leave.

The captain and his entourage gathered the evidence and took their time in leaving the house, walking out like a slow wagon train, with the captain acting as caboose. The photographers gathering up their equipment were the last to leave.

"This is a setup! I didn't kill them. You must believe me," Lizzie pleaded to Emma as soon as the door shut.

Emma hugged her sister. "I believe you."

"We know who's responsible for this!" Bridget was still watching the door. Her hands were at her waist, and her chest heaved with anger. "They murdered your parents and planted everything. The hatchets and the bucket of rags. Everything. They won't get away with this." Her rage caused her Irish accent to be more pronounced.

Emma rose from her chair, walked to the parlor window, and lifted the curtain to peek outside. There were two officers at the wooden gate standing watch. She quickly ran to the kitchen, passing the bloody couch on the way, and peeked out the back window. There was another officer stationed near the barn. "They have officers planted outside," she announced. "Are they here to keep us safe or to spy on us?" she wondered to herself.

Bridget was busying herself with preparing supper and tidying up the kitchen and dining area, while Lizzie and Emma sipped tea and mourned at the dining-room table. They were covered in black from their stockings to the lace veils resting on their heads. No one said a word since the police and reporters left over two hours ago. The smell of roast mutton roamed through the house, slowly replacing the odor of iron-filled blood. Emma stood to serve herself more tea when the bell rang at the front door. Bridget, who was setting places at the table, put down the silverware and napkins she was holding and went to see who was calling at this hour.

"Maybe it's Uncle John," Emma calmly said as she refilled her tea from a porcelain kettle. "He said he would be returning tonight."

Concluding from Emma's comment that it was the girls' uncle, Bridget opened the door without inquiring who was calling and was greeted by a small woman with black hair kept in a bun over a thin face with a small pointy nose in the center.

"Good evening, Bridget." It was Alice Russell, a close friend of Lizzie's. "I see that Fall River has left their finest men behind to keep watch," she said, rolling her eyes toward the two policemen standing guard at the gate.

"Well, they're doing a horrible job if you're here," Bridget stated sarcastically, with a stony expression on her face.

"Nice to see you too," Alice playfully responded as she passed Bridget and headed into the house. "Where are the girls?"

Bridget gestured toward the dining room, and Alice shuffled in, carrying a carpetbag in one arm and a bag of groceries in the other. She set the bags down as Lizzie and Emma stood to welcome her, and the three embraced while Alice offered them her condolences. Bridgett entered the room and took possession of Alice's bags. She put the groceries in the kitchen and the carpetbag with Alice's luggage in a Lizzie's room.

Thirty minutes later, the women were sitting quietly at the dining table finishing the evening's supper. "The turnips were delicious, Maggie." Lizzie broke the silence.

"Yes. Yes. Delicious," Emma and Alice politely agreed in unison.

"Thank you. That's very kind of you," Bridget said as she wiped her mouth with a cloth napkin and rose to clear the table.

"Sit. Please." Lizzie waved her hand toward Bridget's seat at the table. "We can all help with the dishes after."

After what? Bridget thought to herself as she placed her bottom on the chair and reached for her cup of tea.

Lizzie placed her folded hands in front of her on the table, and with the calm of a glassy ocean on a windless day, she explained how they were going to proceed. First, she was going to cooperate with the investigation as she had nothing to hide while the rest of the women, apart from Emma, Bridget, and Alice, would maintain their distance. The motive behind this decision was twofold. The main purpose was to keep the women and their families out of harm's way, and the second was to give the impression that the women had cut ties with Lizzie and Emma, allowing their adversaries to believe that the group was being disbanded and their work had come to an end.

After which, the women would take the opportunity to engage in their own unhindered investigation into the murders, while the attention of the entire town was focused on Lizzie.

Emma and Bridget gave a doubtful look as Alice shook her head in worry.

"What choice do we have?" Lizzie pleaded as she rose from her seat to stretch her legs. "I'm trapped here. They're going to be watching me day and night." She pointed toward the front door in the direction of the sentries stationed outside to stress the point.

"Are you certain? Emme spoke up. "Do you truly believe that you'll get a fair trial? They have the police in the palm of their hands. Who's to say it's not the same with the judges. You heard Mr. Cross. He said those things have friends everywhere. They'll put you away for life in some prison, or worse, in one of those asylums."

Lizzie returned to her seat and shrugged away her sister's concerns. Although in her heart she knew that Emma had good reason to fear for Lizzie's well-being, as it was a customary solution to have women whose behavior contradicted their assigned roles as submissive, silent partners to be diagnosed with lunacy and put away. It was a very simple process that required only one thing. The testimony of any male citizen who desired to have a woman committed because he felt insulted, or insecure, as a result of her independent behavior. If a woman demanded that she be treated as an equal or was too interested in any books other than the Bible, than she could be sent to an asylum for as long as it took her to regain her senses. And she was being accused of much more than that.

The women sat quietly for a moment, until Lizzie broke the silence and reached for Emma and Bridget's hands. They joined hands with Alice, and the group recited the Lord's Prayer. Bridget wrapped it up with a Hail Mary, which made the protestant ladies feel uncomfortable, yet they continued to hold hands out of respect for their colleague.

*****

For the next week the Borden sisters' peace of mind and privacy were subjected to the pandemonium of an investigation and the increased traffic of onlookers who came to see the Murder House of Fall River. They posed for photographs in front of the house. Sometimes accompanied by the officers who were guarding the premises.

The police spent the next few days questioning Lizzie and those who were on the premises at or around the time of the murders, trying desperately to pin the crime on her. They talked with John Morse, an uncle of Lizzie's and Emma's, who happened to be visiting to discuss financial opportunities with Andrew Borden, who stated that he was out of the house at the time and had not returned until later that afternoon. They also spoke with Mrs. Churchill, a neighbor who happened by and discovered the bodies with Lizzie and Bridget, but she only told them what they already knew. She went to the Bordens to see if the girls were going to attend the weekly Bible Study and was shocked by what she found. When they questioned Bridget, they got even less.

On August 8, just two days after her father's funeral, Lizzie's extensive interrogation began. The grief from her father's murder was still fresh, and she cried uncontrollably throughout the questioning. And she only provided misleading and contradictory statements or nothing at all during the many hours of the grueling interviews.

The issue of insanity was raised, and they began administering morphine on a regular basis to help her calm her nerves. From that point on, her mind was muddled, and her statements became incoherent. There was no point in continuing.

Furthermore, when they spoke with the other neighbors and individuals who were in the area at the time, no one saw or heard a thing. No one was spotted entering or leaving the Borden house. The investigation was leading nowhere. There was no sign of a sexual assault on either of the bodies, and nothing was taken from the house, which excluded robbery as a motive. However, the details of the murders implied that they were done in house, and all roads led to Lizzie.

The well-designed conspiracy was going according to plan, and Ms. Borden was taken into custody on August 11, one week after her parents' murder. Lizzie, Emma, and Andrew Jennings, an attorney, were in the parlor reviewing legal documents and trying to disregard the throngs of people crowding the sidewalk and street in front of their home, when the doorbell rang. Bridget descended the stairs to answer the door. She was holding an armful of fresh linens.

"Who is it," she asked.

"Captain Desmond," A man's voice responded. "I'm sorry for the inconvenience, ma'am. But…we're here for Ms. Elizabeth."

Bridgett switched the linens to her other arm and opened the door. The captain was standing at the threshold, adjusting his belt under his waistline, accompanied by the officer who brought the hatchets up from the basement during the previous search. Mayor Coughlin and City Marshal Hilliard were standing behind them. The Marshal was smirking and holding a document close to his lapel.

Bridget patiently stepped aside. "Ms. Borden, we have guests again," she announced.

The city marshal shoved his way to the front and stomped into the parlor, briskly holding out his hand with the documents. "This is a warrant for your arrest for the murders of Andrew and Abby Borden."

Lizzie and Emma stood up, showing no emotion, while Bridget observed the scene from the entryway. Andrew Jennings placed himself between the ladies and the Marshal. He grabbed the documents from the Marshal and skimmed them as thoroughly as possible and turned to Lizzie. He nodded solemnly with a long blink, confirming that the warrant was authentic. Lizzie held her hands out, and Captain Desmond approached her to place the manacles on her.

At that moment, Mayor Coughlin stepped forward. "They'll be no need for that," he grumbled through his thick mustache. "Ms. Borden won't be giving us any more trouble." His sarcastic leer implied that he was part of the whole scheme, and he wanted her to know. He stretched his hand out to her like a courtly gentleman, but she ignored his offer and walked past him, followed by her sister. When they reached the entryway, Bridget turned to join them, and they walked out the front door with their adversaries trailing behind them.

Once the group exited the house, they were hailed with jeers and cheers from the mass of people who were gathered on the street to witness the momentous event. The arrest of the Fall River Killer.

There was a black carriage parked along the sidewalk waiting to transport Lizzie to jail. It was barely visible behind the shouting mob of people in attendance, and a path had to be cleared. The captain blew a whistle, and several policemen appeared pushing and shoving at the crowd until there was a clearing from the gate of the Borden property to the carriage wide enough to allow the group to pass through.

The crowd complained and shouted at the officers, momentarily ceasing their protests. Some of the spectators had already decided that Lizzie was guilty, and they were there to express their outrage toward her, while others were there to pray for her salvation. Yet many of them, much to the displeasure of Mayor Coughlin and the Marshal Hilliard, were there in support of Lizzie and chanting for her freedom.

"Hurry along now, Ms. Borden," Captain Desmond urged with a shove while fending off probing hands from the gauntlet of protesters.

Out of spite for her supporters, the mayor and the marshal immediately merged themselves between Lizzie and her company, leaving Bridget and Emma to be engulfed by the large crowd. An officer opened the door, and Lizzie climbed onto the carriage. But instead of stepping inside, she turned to address the crowd, and they instantly grew silent in anticipation of her announcement.

She eyed the crowd and rested her gaze on Emma and Bridget. Alice was standing next to them, wiping tears from her eyes. She had shown up during the arrest and, with the determination of a mother bear, made her way through the mob.

"The footprints of Jesus that make the pathway glow, we will follow the steps of Jesus wherever they go," she declared with ferocity and pointed an index finger at her temple. Emma and Bridget gave the slightest of nods in recognition of the coded gesture, while Alice continued to cry.

Upon hearing the familiar phrase, the masses rung out in unison, "Sweetly, Lord, have we heard thee calling. Come follow me! And we see where thy footprints falling, lead us to thee."

At the sound of the impromptu chorus, Lizzie lifted her shoulders with confidence and leered at the mayor, giving him the implication that she was well aware that he was involved in her parents' murder. His brow furrowed in anger, and he and the marshal pushed forward, forcing Lizzie inside the carriage. The captain shut the door behind them. She took a seat and Detective Seaver, who was waiting in the carriage, was facing her with his hands folded in his lap. He greeted her, and the carriage rolled away, escorted by the sound of an angelic chorus singing in praise of Lizzie. The martyr of Fall River.

*****

The carriage pulled up in front of the train station, and the group exited the carriage and waited for the next train departing for Taunton. It was a little before three o'clock in the afternoon, and the depot was unusually crowded as protesters added to the congestion of the regular travelers.

Edwin A. Buck, reverend of the Central Congregational Church, and an ardent supporter of Lizzie, was waiting on the platform to join them. His thick, bushy goatee reflected the afternoon sunlight as he stood patiently with his hands at his sides. Behind him was a flock of parishioners holding Bibles and banners, protesting Lizzie's arrest and incarceration.

"What is he doing here?" Mayor Coughlin sneered at Marshal Hilliard.

"It's a free country," Detective Seaver sighed smoothly while surveying the premises for any suspicious activity. His right hand was under his coat, resting on the butt of his revolver.

"He's nothing but a muckraker if you ask me," the mayor complained.

"Who's asking?" the detective said bluntly.

The mayor gave him a sideways look. "Well, they better keep their distance," he complained again while he leered at the group of protesters.

The reverend approached the group and solemnly addressed them before walking up to Lizzie and taking her hands in his. "Have they been treating you well, my dear?" he asked her.

The mayor mumbled something under his breath and attempted to separate Lizzie and the reverend, but they wouldn't be budged. The train taking them to Taunton pulled into the station, and the mayor took pride in announcing that it was time for Lizzie, Marshall Hilliard, and Detective Seaver to board with the intention of dismissing the reverend.

"Yes, we should board," the reverend concurred with a smile, still holding Lizzie's hands.

"The kind reverend has agreed to accompany me today," Lizzie stated flatly while the mayor and the marshal's expressions went from confused to disappointed.

The mayor escorted them to the train and bid farewell to Marshal Hilliard and Detective Seaver, who boarded the train with Lizzie and the reverend. From there, she was transported to Taunton, where large crowds of spectators and supporters had assembled at the train station and in the streets in hopes of catching a glimpse of the infamous Lizzie Borden.

"I saw her! I saw her!" a teenage boy exclaimed almost jumping out of his overalls.

"She smiled at me!" a little girl standing next to him cried, and she shoved the boy playfully. The two turned and made their way through the thick crowd, yelling after their parents. "We saw her!"

Inside the carriage, Lizzie gleamed with delight and waved to her supporters like a queen, while the marshal and the detective sat in silence staring at her. The reverend was next to her, reading a pocket-sized Bible and brushing his silver goatee with his hand.

They arrived at the Bristol County jail in Taunton, and the marshal handed Lizzie over into the custody of Sheriff Wright, who happened to be a native of Fall River; it was rumored that he and his wife were acquaintances of Andrew and Abby Borden. Before departing, Reverend Edwin embraced Lizzie and advised her to keep the faith. "They're afraid of you," he told her and gave a hope-filled smile.

Lizzie said goodbye and permitted the sheriff to lead her into her new residence at the lockup. The buildings were situated at the intersection of Chandler Avenue and Hodges Avenue, near the Taunton State Hospital. On the outside, the facility had the appearance of a university with quaint shaded walkways bordered by landscaped gardens amid ivy-covered buildings. Lizzie's spirits were raised by the scenery, but they suddenly dropped at the sight of the state hospital as it reminded her of the real possibility of her being declared insane and committed against her will. She knew in her heart that the evidence in the case would go in her favor and that justice would prevail, but there was always a chance that her enemies would use the prejudiced mental health system against her to protect themselves.

She entered the facility escorted by Sheriff Wright and the prison turnkey Granville Carter. Once they passed through the entryway, the commotion from the spectators outside was dampened by the brick-walled building heightening the sensation of separation from society, causing Lizzie's spirits to drop even more. After the mandatory bath and delousing, they guided her to the cell, and she paused before entering to examine her living quarters. It was furnished with a tin wash-basin stand, a single chair, and a bed with a lumpy hair mattress. The hefty door was reinforced with iron bars, and above the bed there was a grated window that permitted very little light to enter. She stepped inside, and the turnkey closed the iron door behind her.

"Supper is served at five thirty," the sheriff informed her through the iron bars of the door.

She gave a hearty sigh and set her belongings on the bed, which consisted of a Bible, stationary, and a spare change of clothes. Then she lifted her dress, knelt beside the chair, and folded her hands in prayer. "Our father, who art in heaven..."

CHAPTER 11

Framed

For the next ten months up until her trial began in June, Lizzie occupied her time with reading her Bible and writing letters to friends and supporters when she wasn't busy performing the required chores of an inmate.

She kept to herself and avoided speaking with other inmates, as well as the guards, because she had no idea who their ears belonged to. As far as she was concerned, everyone from the jailer and the sheriff to the lawyers and judges lived in the pockets of her enemies. Even the people serving her food could not be trusted. So she maintained her sanity and her nourishment with supplies and food provisions from the courtesans that were filtered to her through church groups and anonymous supporters.

*****

"The courtesans. Alright! Now were getting somewhere." Henry was sitting with his back against the reception counter and licking his lips. He had just finished another peach.

Varick was lying down a few feet away and staring at the ceiling as he told his tale. "It was around this time that they took the name and declared themselves a private social club. Their headquarters was based at Elizabeth Borden's Maplecroft Estate," he explained briefly.

"Maplecroft?" Henry questioned while digging through his net-ful of produce for another snack.

"It was a property that Ms. Borden purchased after her father's death with the benefit of her inheritance," Varick told Henry and then went on to tell his story.

*****

The turnkey and the guards took measures to put pressure on Lizzie and make her time in jail as unbearable as possible. They started by limiting her visitors to family and making her empty the trash and slop buckets of the other inmates in her section of the jail. She shrugged off their feeble attempts at crushing her hopes and calmly accepted the consequences of the game they were playing.

Her weekly visits from her sister Emma, and her faith in God, kept her in good spirits. Since her guests were regulated to family members, the only visitor she received was Emma. Her cousins, and fellow courtesans, Anna and Carrie were being forbidden by their parents from associating with Lizzie. During the visits, Lizzie and Emma would be allowed to take walks about the facility, but they were always accompanied by prison guards who were paid to eaves-drop and monitor their conversations, which led to them having to speak in code.

Lizzie's correspondences were being monitored as well. Every letter that she wrote and every letter that arrived for her was read thoroughly by the guards for anything that could be used against her in the trial. She was wise to their methods and had taken the proper precautions. She made sure to keep her correspondences as bland as possible and only wrote to individuals who had no association with her or any of the other courtesans and were far removed from the horrible incident. In some of her letters, she would hint at the dispar-ity of her situation, knowing that the guards were drooling over them and would convey those details to their benefactors, giving them the impression that they were breaking her.

Other letters were written to members of various women's rights groups and passed on to the courtesans. These letters were written in code using Bible scriptures, chapters, and page numbers to conceal their genuine content: developments in the investigation into who was responsible for the murder of Lizzie's parents and the movements and whereabouts of their accursed targets.

Thus was her existence up until the time when she was transferred to the Ash Street jail on June 3 and held there for the duration of the trial.

*****

Back in Fall River the haves and have-nots, newly arrived immigrants, and previous settlers all worried for their safety and grew into the habit of looking over their shoulders and entering their homes armed and with extreme caution. Many in Fall River still believed that Elizabeth was innocent and feared that the true killer still lurked about. This fear was reinforced not only by the bodies being discovered around town courtesy of the courtesans, but also by a gruesome murder that occurred on May 30 while Elizabeth was incarcerated.

The killing took place on a dairy farm on the outskirts of Fall River, and the details were very similar to the Borden murders. The slaughter was committed in the morning hours, and the victim, Bertha Manchester, was found in her home with her skull battered. It was also discovered that the murder weapon was an axe, and when this piece of information spread through Fall River, it rejuvenated the panic in the city.

*****

In the meantime, Emma, Bridget, and the Shrove girls intentionally remained out of the spotlight while Felicity took charge of the group and continued to investigate and pester the business interests that served as cogs in the machine of their immortal enemy's empire. However, on account of the activities of the courtesans and the publicity of the trial, their nemesis was engaging in damage control and tying up loose ends, so their efforts were mostly in vain.

Their frustration was growing at the thought of Lizzie rotting in jail while they were getting nowhere, so they decided to visit their old friend Mr. Cross, who owed them a favor since the night he got caught with his pants down in the whorehouse.

Felicity and Deborah were huddled together at the riverbank across from the Barnard Mills Building, observing the glow of light from his office window. The river water splashed behind them and lapped onto the shore.

"He's there," Deborah said.

"Perfect. He has some explaining to do," Felicity replied. She was massaging the iron cross attached to her steel rosary. Each were wearing black cloaks with their white ropes and other useful tools concealed underneath. Constance and Alice were two buildings down, keeping watch, both wearing black cloaks as well.

"Okay. Let's go," Felicity ordered. They rose to cross the road and headed for the Mills Building when someone exited the building and stood on the sidewalk like they were awaiting a carriage. It was a tall, thin individual wearing a long brown coat with matching riding boots and a brown derby pulled down low over their brow, allowing the shadows to cover their face. The figure surveyed the area for a moment before swiftly cutting to its right and darting down the street with amazing speed. It appeared to be carrying a bowling ball in its right hand.

Felicity and Deborah gave each other a desperate look. "Was that one of them?" Deborah asked excitedly.

"We have to follow him," Felicity stressed while searching for Constance and Alice. She placed her fingers to her mouth and blew a high whistle. Two dark shapes emerged from beneath the canopy of a nearby building and raced toward the riverbank.

Deborah reached for Felicity's arm. "But what about Mr. Cross?"

As soon as she spoke, Constance landed next to them along the riverbank, followed by Alice. "What is it? Is he here?" Constance was massaging the bump on the bridge of her nose as she questioned Felicity.

The group climbed the riverbank and ran across to the Mills Building, stopping at the entrance. Felicity quickly explained the tall stranger to the others and ordered Constance to deal with Mr. Cross and meet them back at the church at midnight. After which, she and Alice and Deborah sped after their quarry.

Their chase led them through the city's business district, where they spotted their target several blocks away, running down Pleasant Street, veering left on Main. When they reached the corner of Pleasant and Main, the figure was running swiftly up Anawan Street heading toward the bay area while the distance between them increased because of the uncanny speed of the target. They continued the pursuit until the quarry went off course and moved south into a field of tall grass.

"This way. Hurry!" Deborah whispered, and the others followed.

They made a left down Summer Street and raced toward Spring, hoping to close the distance on the target. Summer was more of an alley than a street. It stretched a short distance between Anawan and Spring Streets and was not as broad as a road. The three dashed through as quickly as possible, working their way around a mass of boys and young men hovering over a square wooden enclosure about three feet high. The yelps and barks of puppies combined with the screeches and squeaks of rodents could be heard under the cheering of the men and boys as they passed the crowd. Many of them holding meager bundles of money.

"Rat-baiting degenerates," Deborah mumbled to herself.

The women exited Summer and went east on Spring Street, which came to an end where the railroad tracks cut across to Elm Street, separating them from their prey. By this time, they were gasping for air and had to pause to catch their breath. After they were reenergized by a second wind, they started the chase once again, but when they reached the train tracks there was no sign of the target. The women grew disheartened for a moment as they thought they had lost him, but then Alice glimpsed a dark shape speeding from a group of trees toward Crab Pond. "Look, there he is," she anxiously pointed out.

*****

The moonlight glared across the water and quivered along with the tiny ripples created by overeager fish jumping at the mosquitos resting on the pond's surface. Bug-eyed bullfrogs were croaking in protest at the fish for not leaving any of the tasty morsels for them as Mayor Coughlin stood under a grove of trees near the northeastern edge of the pond just a few feet away from another man. He was nervously tapping his cane on the ground, showing his impatience, and attempting to assert dominance while the other remained stoic.

"I thought I was to be meeting with Arien." The mayor gave a restless sigh, glanced at his gold pocket watch, and placed it back in his vest pocket. The other man offered no response other than an impassive gaze. He was of average height with light-brown hair and pale skin that blended with the light of the moon as it crossed his boyish face. His beige tweed suit fit him like a glove and accentuated the imposing length of his arms.

"My valet is expecting my return shortly," the mayor firmly stated.

The other man ignored his petty complaints and continued to glare at the mayor with brown eyes whose color swirled around in their corneas, changing shades in whirlpool patterns to reflect the tone of his hair and his well-tailored suit.

Several seconds passed when the man finally spoke. "Ah, here she is," he said and smiled wide to greet the newcomer. His voice swooned like an enticing melody, catching Mayor Coughlin off guard.

The mayor looked around to see who he was referring to and found no one, yet when his attention returned to the brown-eyed man, there was a tall woman in riding clothes and a brown derby at his side. She had wiry, jet-black hair that popped out from under her derby and reached her chin with skin as pale as the other ones.

At the sight of the newcomer, the mayor straightened his jacket and grumbled to the two characters in front of him. "What is this? Where's Arien? Who are you?" he said as he pointed his cane at the pair.

The brown-eyed man placed his hands in the front lower pockets of his tweed jacket and paid the mayor no mind as he greeted the new arrival. "Duna," he said with a nod.

The woman bowed slightly. "I was being followed, but I lost them," she reported.

"Was it those fusty-lug ratbags?" The sound of disgust in his voice contradicted the expressionless look on his smooth face.

"Who else could it have been? If you would just let me…" she was about to express herself when Brown Eyes raised a hand, and she quickly sealed her lips.

*****

"He's a woman!" Deborah said in between breaths. Her chest was heaving from the sprint across the open field. She and Alice were lying on their bellies in the muddy shoreline of the pond, observing the meeting from a safe distance, and waiting for the signal to move in and strike. Felicity was approaching from the opposite end, cautiously working her way through the grove of trees toward the three conspirators, trying her best to stay undetected.

"The other one is in charge," Alice observed out loud when she noticed the woman in the brown derby stiffen when the other one raised his hand.

"This could be our lucky night," Deborah whispered. "He may be the one we've been looking for. Be careful, Felicity." She prayed, holding her steel rosary in her hands.

*****

"Is it done?" the brown-eyed man questioned the woman, without looking away from Mayor Coughlin.

"As ordered," she said flatly, showing no emotion. She stood with her hands behind her back and her eyes on the mayor as well.

The mayor wiped sweat from his upper lip while nervously turning to look behind him and tried uttering something, when the brown-eyed man raised his hand again and cut him off.

"And our uninvited guest?" he folded his hands in front of him at the waist as he asked this question.

The woman smiled at the mayor and brought her arms forward to reveal a severed head she was concealing behind her back. She lifted her chin and raised the head over her mouth, allowing what was left of the blood to drip into her mouth. After which, she tossed the head at the feet of the mayor and wiped her mouth with the sleeve of her coat. "His brain still lives. Quite delicious" was all she said.

Thaddeus! No!" the mayor cried out as his knees gave way beneath him. "You animals. The others will hear about this," he threatened as he regained his footing and started walking backward, attempting to make his escape. A soft breeze swept past him, and he bumped into what he thought was a tree. He turned to see Duna standing directly behind him, blocking his escape, and probing him with the yellow eyes of a wolf. He made a very unimpressive display of bravado. "You'll pay for this."

"His death is on your hands, Mr. Coughlin?" Brown Eyes said nonchalantly, without a hint of concern as he glided toward Mayor Coughlin. "Were you not given specific instructions to come alone?" he said while shaking his head in disapproval like a parent scolding a three-year-old.

He continued to move forward until he was a palm's width away from the mayor, sandwiching the mayor between him and Duna. The mayor could feel his breath cover his face. It was cooler than the outside air and had a soothing effect, causing the mayor to loosen his grip on his cane until it hit the floor.

"Arien will not be coming tonight. He has no time for the likes of you. It is because of you and your colleague, Mr. Cross, that his brother Adrianus is no longer with us." His voice coated the mayor's body like a tranquil waterfall. "And in answer to your question," Brown Eyes stated as the mayor remained calm, entranced by the sound of his voice, "my name is Splinter. I am the solution to the problem. Apparently, you mortals are too feeble-minded to extinguish this fire." He sighed in exasperation. "I warned Arien and Adrianus time and again about your kind."

The mayor tried to talk, but his tongue grew fatter with each attempt, and drool started to build up in the corners of his mouth.

Splinter studied his vacant eyes for a second. "Primitive apes," he spit in disgust and looked over Mayor Coughlin's shoulder at Duna. He turned and walked away from the mayor, whistling the most popular melody of the day, "Lizzie Borden took an axe…"

*****

Felicity concealed herself in the forest grove and eavesdropped on the clandestine conversation. Her back was pressed against a burly tree, whose branches draped over her like furry spider legs. She was clutching tightly to a crossbow she held against her chest. "Arien," she said to herself, making sure to remember the name. "He's the leader." She braced herself to act and whispered a short prayer. "Lord, guide my arrows. For Lizzie."

*****

Duna gently rested her hand on the mayor's back. His hypnotic state prevented him from moving. She opened her mouth and glided her tongue across her fangs in anticipation of a third supper. Mr. Cross's blood tasted of lard and cigars, while the mayor's valet had the flavor of potatoes and ale. She couldn't wait to see what this thin, sweaty, and bearded man would have to offer. She neared his throbbing jugular vein when an odor caught her attention. As she raised her nose to the air, an arrow pierced through her neck and ripped her throat open.

Splinter heard a gushing sound in the background and assumed it was Mayor Coughlin struggling at the hands of Duna and he paused to enjoy the scene of her handiwork. She took her feeding seriously.

However, when he turned to observe the display, he was shocked to find Duna grasping at an arrowhead protruding from her neck as she spewed blood onto the mayor's back. There was a dark cloak approaching fast from the right, holding a small crossbow in front of it. Duna spun on her heels and tore the arrow from her neck, leaving a gaping hole where blood poured out by the gallon. She attempted to walk forward toward the approaching figure, but she was weakened by the enormous loss of blood, and she fell to her knees, holding her neck. The hooded cloak flew past her like a black raven, leaving an arrow between her eyes, and raced straight to Splinter. Duna fell to the ground, smashing her bloody face in the dirt. Her brown derby landed next to her a second later.

In an instant, Felicity's crossbow was slapped away from her hands, and it landed with a crash against an elm tree, breaking apart as it fell to the ground. Before she knew it, there was a long-fingered hand wrapped around her throat and another around her hands. The long fingers flung her to the floor like a rag doll, and she hit the back of her head on a tree root as she landed. The hood to her cloak was thrown back, exposing her face, and when she opened her eyes all she could see were stars.

Splinter studied her for a moment as she wrestled to gain her senses, admiring her auburn hair and pouty lips. "Young fool," he chided as he descended upon her. He reached out to take hold of her when his hand was knocked away and jerked backward while what felt like an iron chain whipped around his neck and tightened like a boa constrictor.

"You brought friends," he strained and smiled wide, exposing salivating fangs.

He swung his arm sideways, and Alice flew in the air several meters landing in the pond. Deborah yanked on the steel rosary wrapped around Splinter's neck and closed in on him from behind. She hopped on top of him and planted her feet in his back and leaned backward to put all her weight into the effort. He unwound Alice's steel rosary from around his forearm and threw it aside as he stretched his arms backward, grabbing Deborah by the wrists, and started pulling her over his head like a loose sweater.

Felicity shook away her headache, jumped to her feet, and saw that Deborah was fighting a losing battle as she clung desperately to Splinter. She ran toward them and took two giant steps before leaping into the air while reaching underneath her cloak.

Splinter had control of the situation when he was briefly distracted by the sound of flapping wings. He looked up onto the sky and saw Felicity falling like a black-winged angel, holding a wooden stake and a hammer in her hands. The stake landed true, and the hammer followed through with a clank and smashed the stake halfway into Splinter's chest. He let out a frightful screech and swiped an arm at her, heaving her against the mayor who was still standing catatonic, causing them both to fall to the ground. Splinter fell backward as well, landing on top of Deborah as he tore frantically at his chest, trying to dislodge the wooden stake.

Felicity watched him fight for his life and glanced at the other half of the stake in her hand. It had broken off when Splinter tossed her aside, leaving nothing for him to grab onto.

His body wrenched and wiggled as he ripped his tweed vest and Egyptian cotton shirt into shreds, trying to get at the stake, allowing Deborah to sneak out from under him. She moved quickly and rose to her feet and backed away slowly from Splinter, as he tore into his chest with his long fingers, digging a hole around the stake. Blood splashed about his torso until his frenzy slowed, and his body began to flatten, making his well-tailored tweed suit seem oversized. His face sunk, and his smooth skin tightened around his skull until it was translucent.

Felicity and Deborah stood over the grotesque sight and offered a small prayer for the damned. The sound of a cracking branch cut their prayer short. They turned with daggers in hand and saw Alice walking toward them, wringing water from her hair.

"Well, I guess they threw the baby out with the bathwater," she quipped, and the others laughed along with her, making light of the situation. Their comic relief was interrupted by the sound of blubbering coming from the mayor, who was sitting on the floor with his legs spread before him. The glossy look in his eyes was fading as the spell of the vampire was waning with Splinter's death.

"What…where am I?" he mumbled through the drool on his lips.

The women were gathered around him, observing his pitiful condition, while he studied his surroundings. His eyes widened in shock at the carnage laid out before him. Duna was lying facedown on the ground with a bloody arrow in her hand and one sticking out the back of her skull, while Splinter's emaciated body was bubbling underneath his tweed suit. Mayor Coughlin trembled with terror when he realized what had taken place and looked up at the women surrounding him. "What have you done?"

*****

Mayor Coughlin was sitting in a chair placed in the center of the church basement, struggling with his guilty conscience and looking down at his twiddling thumbs. The presence of the large cross hanging above the upright piano hovered over him and made him feel like he was about to be given his last rights. He trembled as he lifted his hand to wipe away a stray tear on his cheek.

"We saved your life tonight. Your only option lies with us," Felicity stressed to him. She sat on the bench across from him set in front of the piano, forcing him to look in the direction of the cross. "Our enemies are now your enemies, and you have nowhere to turn."

The mayor whimpered at the last statement while Alice and Deborah stood with arms folded, scrutinizing his behavior. He shook his head in denial, refusing to come to terms with his predicament. "No. No. This isn't happening." His mustache was soaked with drool and tears. "They said… They promised…" he sniveled.

"You made a deal with the devil. What did you think would happen?" Deborah berated him. "Have you not read Faust?"

The sound of the door caught their attention, and the woman turned to find Constance entering the basement. She pulled back the hood to her cloak and let loose her strawberry-blond hair. "He's dead."

"What?" the women declared in sequence, unintentionally imitating an echo.

"Mr. Cross," Constance replied flatly. "He was dead when I got to his office. His body was hanging on a coatrack like a wet blanket. There was no blood in his veins when I checked his pulse," she explained without a trace of remorse. She walked to the back of the room to pour herself a cup of water from a porcelain pitcher that sat on a small table in a corner.

"Curse them!" Felicity said in frustration.

"Sebastian is dead?" Mayor Coughlin bawled, placing his hands over his mouth, trying to keep the vomit in his mouth.

The women were repulsed at the image of the mayor's regurgitated dinner pouring over his hands and seeping through his fingers. Alice ran to the corner table for a napkin and threw it at the whimpering mayor. A few minutes passed, and his sniffling lessened while he cleaned himself up as best as he could. After which he straightened his posture and folded his hands in his lap like a dignified politician preparing to negotiate with a worthy opponent.

"It appears that the ball is in your court, ladies," he said calmly, betraying the fact that only moments ago he was about to soil his pants.

"I don't play tennis, Mr. Coughlin," Felicity responded and crossed her legs, placing her hands on her lap, preparing for their discussion. She then went on to explain to him how he was going to guarantee Lizzie's freedom in exchange for their protection and support against the demonic monstrosities that have entrenched themselves in Fall River, playing its citizens like pawns in their accursed game.

The mayor agreed to lead the investigation into the murder of Lizzie's parents astray and to muddy up the waters of the case, assuring a mistrial. Additionally, he vowed that he and his associates would reveal every detail about the secret cabal of demons who were now a threat to their own lives. In return, his family and the other prominent families who resided on the hill would be kept out of harm's way courtesy of the courtesans.

Following their negotiation, the mayor rose to his feet and offered Felicity his hand to seal the deal. She remained seated and held out a limp hand, implying that the mayor would do better by kissing her hand out of respect. He frowned at the idea of being put in his place by this upstart, but as she explained to him while she twisted her braided hair in her other hand, "You have nowhere to turn." He bowed forward, took her hand in his, gave it a small peck, and dropped it like a hot potato.

Felicity gave him an annoyed look. "Your carriage is parked outside, but you will have to drive yourself," she informed him and waved him away as she spun on the bench and started tapping at the piano keys in front of her.

The mayor started for the door when Deborah stepped in front of him and blocked his path. "Remember, Mayor," she told him in all seriousness. "If you have a change of heart and renege on our agreement, you'll have more to fear than vampires." She held the door open for him, and he exited the basement with his tail tucked beneath his legs.

*****

Mayor Coughlin drove himself home with difficulty as he contemplated the words of the pointy-shouldered woman. It had been years since he had to operate a carriage or ride a horse without an escort. The temperament of the carriage horses was disagreeable, and the thought of his dead valet brought a tear to his eye. His mind was racing with conflicting thoughts, and he hopelessly tried to make sense of the evening's events.

"Out of the frying pan and into the fire," he said to himself while combing his beard with his fingers. "God help me."

CHAPTER 12

Lizzie Must Be Free By 1893

Lizzie waited outside the Ash Street jail to be transported to the New Bedford Courthouse where her trial would be taking place. It was an imposing structure built in the fashion of most facilities of the time: orphanages, Indian boarding schools, and the burgeoning industrial factories that were intended to control its subjects through the ominous threat of severe punishment. The sound foundation and formidable thick brick walls repelled the elements—sunlight, wind, rain, and snow—while concealing the dubious activities from within. She studied the barred windows and said a short prayer for the inmates behind those reinforced walls.

She was fortunate that she did not have to reside in the main jail because of an overcrowding situation in the women's wing. Therefore, she was housed and remained under constant watch at Sheriff White's house, which was adjacent to the prison property, for the next two weeks.

Although she was placed in much better lodgings than she had expected after her experience at the Taunton lockup, Lizzie still had not grown accustomed to the concept of relinquishing her freedoms. Every decision was made for her. Where she could go, when to bathe, when to sleep, and when and what she ate. It was all done under the supervision and watchful eye of the prison staff. Her only contact with the outside world was via day-old newspapers and letters from supporters.

As she contemplated her present existence, she was reminded of a newspaper article that appeared on the front page of *The Brooklyn Daily Eagle* back in January that since then had been buried by yellow journalism and erased from the minds of the populace.

The headline read, Revolution in Hawaii, and went on to describe what was termed an "uprising of the people" that resulted in the removal of the queen and the creation of a provisional government. The writer explained that the reason for the coup d'état was the present monarch's, Queen Liliuokalani, attempt to enact a new constitution that would prohibit non-Hawaiians from participating in franchise and eliminate the current house of nobles while giving the queen the capacity to appoint new members to the house. This was seen as an affront to the foreign community, who took it upon themselves, with the implied threat of the United States Navy, to act in the name of the people of Hawai'i and depose a tyrannical monarch who would deny them of their natural rights.

Lizzie remembers reading the story and feeling somewhat perplexed and disillusioned as it was her understanding of a monarchy that the sovereign ruler, king, or queen, has the right to amend or introduce a constitution without consequence as supreme authority is bestowed upon them. And it was obvious that the persecuted foreign element described in the article consisted of male descendants of wealthy immigrant settlers from the United States, who were unhappy that their power and influence within the foreign government would be stripped away with the enactment of the new constitution that seemed to take the interests of the citizenry of Hawai'i at heart.

It was this subtle detail of the story that caused her stomach to burn with frustration and fill her heart with sympathy for Liliuokalani. Out of fear of losing their positions, powerful men were attempting to dictate the queen's destiny and destroy the fruits of her labor while portraying her as an unqualified leader simply because she was a woman. Now, nearly six thousand miles away, powerful men, mortal and immortal, whose positions were being threatened by the actions of the courtesans, were dictating Lizzie's destiny and attempting to make her appear feeble-minded and weak simply because she was a woman.

Her transport rolled to a stop in front of the jail, and her escorts prompted her inside. It was an unpainted wooden coach with one iron-barred window in the rear. The coach swayed from side to side like an unsteady lifeboat throughout the long and quiet ride. One of the guards had to reswallow his breakfast several times, and Lizzie mercifully offered him a handkerchief. His comrade cleared his throat in disapproval, and the guard's face reddened with embarrassment while he raised his hand to his mouth and his Adam's apple shifted to allow his regurgitation to slide back down his throat. Lizzie giggled to herself.

As they arrived at the courthouse, a large crowd of supporters as well as dissenters had to be scattered to create enough space for the coach to park and unload its passengers. Cheers and jeers were shouted when Lizzie stepped out of the coach. Her escorts impatiently elbowed their way through the crowd as they led her up the stairs and through the courthouse doors.

The courtroom was at capacity when Lizzie arrived. The benches were clogged with men and women of all classes, some with restless children on their laps, while others stood lining the walls from corner to corner. She scanned the crowd and spotted her sister, Emma, and Maggie sitting in the front row. They were holding hands and dabbing a handkerchief at the tears on their cheeks. A few spaces down, Mayor Coughlin sat nervously with his hat on his lap and his hands folded in front of him. He was sitting uncomfortably between two elegantly dressed ladies wearing large silk hats with black veils covering their faces. One had her arm wrapped around the mayor's, her lace gloves caressing his bicep, while the other stirred the hot summer air in front of her with a handheld fan.

"You're perspiring profusely, Mr. Coughlin," Felicity said as she handed him a handkerchief. Her auburn hair was kept in its usual braid and tucked underneath her silk hat. "Here. Clean yourself up."

She leaned in close to him. "Just relax and keep your word," she whispered. The mayor wiped his forehead and adjusted his collar.

"Don't worry. I have no intention of crossing you…ladies," he fearfully stammered.

Deborah giggled from beneath her black veil, and the mayor gave her a tense look. She straightened her posture, highlighting her broad, pointy shoulders and snapped her fan shut. Mayor Coughlin turned his attention toward the jury box and remained silent, while his associates in the courtroom observed in dismay as they suspected who his companions were.

The crowd hushed when Lizzie took her seat at the defendants' table next to her attorneys Andrew Jackson Jennings and George Robinson, the former governor of Massachusetts. The former governor's presence heightened the mood and everyone, young and old, stared in complete silence as the gravity of the situation dawned upon them that the trial of the decade was about to commence.

*****

The trial began on June 5 and went on for two weeks, much to the chagrin of the immortals and their human counterparts, who intended the trial to end quickly, so that Fall River could put all this messy business behind them and get back to what really mattered. Stability and profit. To accomplish this, they needed to make an example out of Lizzie, which required a verdict of guilty.

Therefore, measures were taken to assure the desired outcome by placing the right-minded individuals on the bench and the jury, which consisted of all men since women were not allowed to serve as jurors because they lacked the right to vote. The result was a grand jury of twelve conspicuously wealthy men from the hill with ties to the financial world. Lizzie was familiar with a few of the faces because some of them had dined at her father's table at one time or another.

She looked them over, studying each one in their three-piece suits adorned with cuff links, pocket watches, and gold rings. They sat there with uninterested looks on their faces as if they all had someplace better to be. A golf course, a hunting lodge, or a bath-house. Her mind flashed back to the article from the *Brooklyn Daily Eagle* about Hawai'i. The article was accompanied by a photo of the men who spearheaded the movement to overthrow the Queen of Hawai'i. Under the photo, a caption read, the *Committee of Safety*. Lizzie joked to herself that the members of the jury strangely resembled the members of the Committee of Safety, and she couldn't help but smile at the irony.

All rose and removed their hats when the three justices for the trial entered the courtroom: Albert Mason, Caleb Blodget, and Justin Dewey, all respected judges. Felicity and Deborah placed their veiled hats in their laps, exposing their faces, and allowing the mayor's associates to confirm their suspicions regarding his new friends. Mayor Coughlin fearfully swallowed a lump in his throat the size of a walnut.

Lizzie's defense team entered a not-guilty plea, which was to be expected, but what wasn't expected was the public friction and the societal division the case would cause. Lizzie was from a well-respected family whose finances and affairs were entrenched in the Fall River establishment. She was a Sunday school teacher and a staunch suffragist. Additionally, many a Fall River housewife were grateful for the courtesans' work at the brothels and taverns that kept their wayward husbands home at night.

The immortals and their associates also weren't prepared for the rallying cries being heard not only in Massachusetts but across the nation as well. The Temperance Movement, Suffragists, and Feminists mustered support for Lizzie, and church groups held prayer vigils day and night. News outlets everywhere condemned the police and attacked their investigation, stating that they were engaging in a witch hunt while publishing articles advocating Lizzie's innocence. Someone was sabotaging their plans to sweep the issue under the rug and move on.

*****

The prosecution team called many witnesses to testify against Lizzie. Including those close to her, hoping to reveal Lizzie's barbarous nature. They called her sister, Emma, to the stand to discuss

Lizzie's relationship with her father counting on some of the rumors in town about Lizzie's disgust for her father's new wife to be true. Yet when she was questioned, all Emma could declare was that Lizzie and her father were very close, and that her father Andrew died wearing a ring that Lizzie had given to him when she was a child. Lizzie teared up at the memory, and the crowd expressed its sympathy through the women in the room dabbing at their own tears with soiled handkerchiefs of their own. District Attorney Knowlton's shoulders dropped just a nudge in disappointment, and he took his seat next to his partner.

When they called on the housekeeper, Bridget, to testify during the line of questioning Felicity and Deborah were watching her closely as some of the courtesans still had their doubts about Maggie because of her Catholic beliefs.

The prosecution focused on her status as an Irish immigrant and tried to intimidate her into turning on Lizzie, but the maneuver fell short of its goal. Bridget held true to her allegiance to Lizzie and the courtesans and testified that she never saw any signs of discord between Lizzie and her stepmother, Abbey. Attorney Moody dismissed her with impatience, and the prosecution decided to try another tactic.

Prior to the beginning of the trial, the propaganda machine under orders from their immortal benefactors were spreading misinformation about Lizzie's mental state during her ten-month incarceration. An article was released by the *Fall River Daily Herald* reporting that Lizzie's "long confinement and approaching trial are unnerving" her and that she was "on the grade down."

The prosecution cited this article and tried everything in their arsenal to claim that she was insane and needed to be institutionalized in a state asylum. They argued that Lizzie showed all the signs of an unstable female, which made her behave in ways that did not conform to society. Furthermore, they proclaimed that her arrogant attitude and defiance were a result of overeducation and that she suffered from suppressed menstruation as well as religious excitement.

This was a direct challenge to Lizzie's character and behavior as her lifestyle went against the sentiments of traditional society. She and the courtesans represented the new ideal of the modern Victorian woman. An educated, professional woman whose life choices consisted of more than having babies and darning socks, and these ideals conflicted with the male ego.

The audience hissed from time to time at these outlandish arguments showing their disapproval of the prosecutor's portrayal of Lizzie. However, when Moody discussed the stability of a woman's mind after losing a loved one the crowd, and the jury paid special attention. Prosecutor Moody explained that because of the fragile construct of the female mind the depression experienced by a woman after the death of a loved one is so enormous that many women never recover, and institutionalization is the only solution. His argument went on to explain that the death of Lizzie's father and stepmother, in combination with her prolonged confinement, have had such an effect on her mental stability that she will have to be monitored consistently for the rest of her life. Hence, commitment to an asylum would be the most humane decision in this case to guarantee Lizzie's safety.

Mumbled comments rolled through the crowd like a soft wave with curious *oohs* and *aahs* cresting the conversations. It was at this point that Lizzie grew concerned about the outcome of the trial and her well-being. She was aware that women basically had no rights when it came to issues of mental health, and that the mental health system was used as a weapon against woman, especially outspoken women, to keep them in line with societal expectations. Any man, blood relative or acquaintance, that was familiar with a woman could express their concerns and have a woman committed for any number of reasons. Accepted symptoms were as trivial as exhaustion, headaches, avoiding household responsibilities, too much interest in sex or too little, or never having been married. And being a single thirty-year-old woman did not fare well for Lizzie in the eyes of the all-male jury.

*****

"Wow, what a trip," Henry stated. "Women couldn't vote, and they could be locked up for anything? Just 'cause someone felt like it? That's messed up"

"Yes. It was very sad," Varick said calmly. "Unfortunately, I've witnessed several episodes in human history that have mirrored one another, although they were hundreds of years apart.

Henry gave Varick a confused look while trying to hold back a yawn. "What do you mean?"

"During the latter half of the seventeenth century, not too far from Fall River, men used stereotypes, popular opinion, and superstitions to suppress women and marginalize their existence. If a husband was unhappy with his wife and wanted to replace her with a younger lover, if there was a selfish brother who coveted the entire family inheritance, or if any man who was jealous of a woman's prosperity and wanted to claim hold of her assets, all one had to do was point to suspicions of witchcraft.

"Witchcraft and lunacy were both used against women for the same purposes. The difference was that being suspected of a witch resulted in death, whereas lunacy led to a lifetime confinement in an asylum."

Varick paused for a second and grinned. "Maybe the witches were lucky," he quipped.

Henry did not respond to Varick's joke. He only stared at him like a child wary of his mother's puns that only she laughs at. "So what happened with the rest of the trial?"

Varick closed his eyes and finished the tale.

*****

Eventually, the prosecution's ardent efforts began to wane with each setback they were dealt. First, the testimony of many of the witnesses called were filled with contradictions and hearsay that left gaps in the prosecution's case. Then the feeble evidence brought forth failed to convince the jurors of Lizzie's involvement with her parents' murder. Including what everyone believed would be the most damning evidence. The scene of the crime.

No matter how hard the prosecutors tried to paint the picture of a gruesome murder scene, the photos and evidence conflicted their claims because of the small amount of blood, not only on or about Lizzie's clothing and the crime scene, but on or about and within the Bordens' bodies themselves. This most interesting detail of evidence made it even more difficult to tie the murders to Lizzie, so it was later swept aside.

Yet Lizzie did not forget this tidbit of information. Her parents were drained of almost all their blood, and she knew why. She also knew why it was suspected that Abbey, her stepmother, was facing her murderer when the incident took place. Because she and Lizzie's father, Andrew, were familiar with their killer, or killers.

In fact, this particular feature wasn't reported by any of the detectives on the scene, but it was noticed by a reporter of a small newspaper, who mysteriously disappeared after his story broke.

In addition, Lizzie's defense team destroyed the lunacy theory by appealing to the sensibilities of the modern woman. They contended that the image set forth by the prosecution regarding Lizzie and her mental health status was a misinterpretation founded on outdated stereotypes and gender roles. They maintained that what some people, mainly men, saw as arrogance was little more than self-confidence, and what the prosecution referred to as overeducation was merely the result of an industrious individual and stated that these same characteristics would be applauded if they were discussing a man. It was then that the jurist and the three judges knew they were presented with a challenge because each one was married and had daughters of their own. Daughters whom they themselves were sending to the best colleges to be educated and learn about the modern world. What would these wives and daughters think if these men decided to put a young woman away simply for being independent minded.

The final nail in the prosecution's coffin was when the three judges declared that the testimony from Lizzie's inquest after the murders was inadmissible because she should have had a lawyer present since she was technically a prisoner being charged with a crime at the time.

Thus, suffering one defeat after another, the prosecution decided to rest their case. This decision in combination with the behind-the-scenes work of Mayor Coughlin to convince the attorney generals along with other prestigious men of commerce of Fall River to intentionally stonewall the legal process as much as possible led to Lizzie's acquittal. It wasn't difficult for the mayor to persuade these men of power to switch loyalties because, unbeknownst to the public, they privately benefitted from the activities of the courtesans. The women were doing them a favor by eliminating their silent partners, who held sway over them and truly pulled the strings from behind the scenes. The vampire community. Hence the acquittal.

*****

Lizzie exited the courthouse with Emma, Maggie, Felicity, and Deborah following close behind. The crowd roared wildly at the sight of her and her cohorts. Emma and Maggie each grabbed Lizzie by the hand and raised them in victory.

"I am the happiest woman in the world," she declared.

Emma and the ladies moved the crowd aside and led Lizzie to a grand double-doored, purple-painted carriage waiting for them at the foot of the steps. They leisured comfortably in the spacious carriage. Maggie sat with her legs spread wide in front of her. Deborah kicked one of her legs to the side.

"Why must you sit like a man? You're taking up all of the space," she added as she adjusted her position. Maggie grumbled and slid her legs closer together.

Lizzie stared out of the window in silence. The others watched her with anticipation. "Now that this business is behind us, we have work to do," she said to them while still gazing out the curtained carriage window. She turned to them and smiled. "Is anyone else hungry?"

Maggie gave a grim smile. "She's back" was all that she said.

CHAPTER 13

Party at Ground Zero

Outside of the forest-covered customer-service building, the dawn's dim light was growing brighter by the minute, and Varick gave a wearisome sigh. "Well, there it is. The genuine story of Lizzie Borden. Satisfied now?"

Henry yawned and nodded his head in answer to Varick's question.

However, after a minute of silence, Varick unexpectedly carried on. "Despite the fact that Lizzie was acquitted and dismissed of all charges, there is still a certain truth to her legend. She was, indeed, a murderer. And many distinguished citizens of Spindle City fell victim to that dreaded woman and her courtesans. This I can attest to." A tinge of anger touched his tone when he said this.

Henry sat up and stretched his arms above his head. "Really?" he asked, before rubbing his eyes, trying to keep the sandman away. "Does this have anything to do with that time you said you met her? What's up with that?" he stated in his usual blunt fashion.

Lost in thought for a moment, Varick gazed at the floor as the memories overwhelmed his mind. "It was an evening near the turn of the century, I believe." Varick began to explain when Henry raised an eyebrow and gave him a questioning glance.

"The nineteenth century?" Varick said like an impatient parent.

"Thank you for clearing that up. I mean, how many times have you experienced a turn of the century, man?" Henry replied.

Varick ignored the comment. He was used to Henry's brashness by now. "Indeed. It was the eighteen nineties," he continued. "Some years after the Borden trial had taken place and I was enjoying a late night supper in the company of friends. Well, not exactly friends, but beings of the same mind if you will."

"You mean other vampires?" Henry inquired with great interest. Eyes wide open as if he had forgotten about his lack of sleep that evening.

"Correct, but no ordinary group of vampires. This was a coven hidden in what was then the Forest of Cape Cod Bay. It was one of the last of its kind in that area that I was aware of. The leader of the nest and proprietor of the estate was a vampire of great importance from Romania, who went by the name of Caliban the Black. He was a tall, menacing figure with one silver eye. He had lost the other against the Byzantium forces in a thirteenth-century battle where he was fighting for the Ottoman Empire. It left him with a scar that went from his eye socket to his ear in a straight line. As coincidence would have it, he arrived in the United States to get things in order after the demise of Adrianus and Arien.

"I myself had recently returned from a brief stint in the Caribbean Islands, and I had been residing at the estate temporarily under the premise that I was a prospective member of their covenant and that I would be joining them for breeding purposes. You see, this particular coven was only interested in pure-blooded, naturally born vampires. Unlike most groups who tolerated the turned, they wanted nothing at all to do with such converts. Although I had no intentions of joining their group."

"No? Why not?" Henry wondered aloud.

"No. During those years I was dealing with certain hardships." Varick somberly expressed. "So I sought others of my kind with the hopes that it would…provide the comforting I needed."

"Hardships?" Henry questioned. "I thought you vamps were perfect through and through. Let me guess? After a thousand years of living, you spotted crow's feet around the eyes, oh me oh my." He placed his palms on the sides of his face and mimicked a pouting clown.

"Your insensitivity never ceases to amaze me," Varick stated while giving Henry a concrete look. "As I was saying, I was there for the company." He paused for a moment. "Yet that's not entirely true I was also seeking information."

"What kind of information?" asked Henry.

Varick responded, not realizing he was subconsciously nodding his head. "There were strange events occurring in the supernatural world, and the temporal world as well, that needed explaining and the coven was the only venue that I felt could provide any answers. Or at the least offer some sort of clue."

Henry was looking at Varick, waiting for an explanation. He was familiar with notions of the supernatural, thanks to his abuela, and he wanted to hear what Varick the vampire considered strange events. Especially since for the past few decades the dead have been freely roaming the planet. There was no explanation. "Did you find any answers?"

Varick gazed out toward the sky's orange hue leaking between the foliage for a moment without responding. "No. No answers, just…breadcrumbs," he said in disappointment.

"Hmm," Henry mused. "Sounds kinda like a movie I saw on the boob tube when I was a kid. There was this vampire looking for answers, just like you were, but he ended up in Paris with a bunch of overly theatrical vampires. He snapped his fingers several times, trying to kickstart his memory. "What was the name of that flick? Something about interviewing the vampire. Yeah, it's like that movie."

Varick let out another sigh. "If that piece of fiction helps you grasp the reality of the situation, then so be it."

"It's just an observation, man. Take it easy. Everyone's tired here," Henry quipped.

"Yes, you seem to be full of observations," Varick sighed, again before continuing. "That night we were feasting in honor of the winter solstice, the longest night of the year. I'm sure you're familiar with some of the anecdotes intended to frighten the young that speak of a night where witches and werewolves come out to play and prey. Well, there's some truth to these tales. I cannot speak for the Wiccan community, nor do I ever enjoy discussing Lycan matters, but we vampires relish this night, and the longer the better. After all…the night belongs to us."

Visions of dance floors packed with people dressed in leather, latex, denim, and the occasional business suit, dancing under a cloud of smoke, while a mysterious dark-haired woman howled at the moon-sized mirror ball spinning above the congregation. *"Because the night belongs to lovers. Because the night belongs to us!"*

"As a matter of fact…" Varick went on once he returned from his vison of grandeur. "I wasn't the only guest in attendance as it was a celebration. There were others from the region that did not belong to the coven, yet were still significant enough to be invited to such an occasion. Humans as well. All arrived bearing gifts, of course, some were accompanied by their personal pets and others by their lovers. In some cases, they were one in the same. Many of the women wore gowns of sheer silk dating from the Kushan empire, while other guests dressed as animals or important figures from history. Some chose the traditional route of evening wear, yet they were adorned most extravagantly, each one trying to outshine the next like restless pimps at a player's ball."

Henry's head jerked toward Varick in surprise. "Did you just say a player's ball?"

Varick gave him a sly smile and kept talking as if Henry never spoke. "The soiree was fantastic, and it was exactly what I needed. I can still smell the sweat and the tears fused with the scent of the other fluids that ooze themselves from our bodies. Glistening forms were everywhere at once, weaving in and out with one another, creating an image akin to intertwined asps in a serpent's nest. It was an all-out orgy. It was electric." He exposed his teeth, fangs and all, with a grin that went from ear to ear. His eyelids were shut, but they were moving from the rolling eyes underneath. "The taste of blood still lingers on the back of my throat. The blood of the humans in attendance that night who wished to emulate us yet unbeknownst to them they were only there to quench our thirsts and satisfy our souls. The evening was going magnificently. Until that woman and her friends showed up." His face went from elation to vexation with the last statement.

*****

"Sounds like they're having a grand time in there," Felicity whispered to the others, while she twisted her auburn braid in her hands.

She was squatting underneath a group of white spruce trees situated several yards across from the front entrance to the estate. A fountain that looked like two angels hugging and a wide gravel path separated the trees from the estate. Three dark shapes squatted next to her.

"Wait until we arrive," Constance said, rubbing the bump along the edge of her nose. It was a memento from when the courtesans were just getting started with their works.

"They're in for a real big surprise," Deborah added.

Alice nodded in agreement. They were all wearing large, hooded cloaks. Large enough to conceal all their weapons: iron rosaries, silver-razor-lined ropes, crossbows, and meat cleavers. There were also a few additions to their arsenal such as grenades filled with silver and mercury and dynamite sticks coated in garlic.

Felicity pulled out a watch from under her cloak. "Any second now," she informed the others. "As soon as we hear the back-entrance breach, we blast the front doors and charge. And remember, no one gets out alive."

Three black hoods nodded in agreement. Felicity focused her attention on the front entrance of the estate. It was a double door at the top of a wide set of stairs that ended in a large portico. There were carved Roman columns on either side of it. At the foot of the door sat two burlap sacks filled with dynamite. Any minute now, Lizzie and the others should be making their way over the wall and toward the back entrance. And then Boom!

*****

"Once we're over that wall, stick to the shadows as practiced and head for the back entrance." Lizzie directed her cousins Carrie and Anna. "Maggie and the others will come over the east wall and enter through the banquet hall." Maggie was positioned near the east wall with the Brayton sisters, Elizabeth and Sarah, waiting with anticipation. Ellen Shrove was stationed across from the front gate, keeping an eye out for any newcomers and readying the concealed carriages for the getaway."

"Remember, no one gets out alive," Lizzie stressed before she lowered herself to one knee and offered her cupped hands as a step to the first courtesan willing to go over the wall.

*****

"Eventually, I became overwhelmed with sensations inside and out, from the ends of the hair on my head to the soles of my feet. I had to come up for air, so I grabbed my garments and walked out to a gazebo located in the center of the rear courtyard. As I was sitting there gathering my senses and taking in the aroma of the gardenias surrounding the gazebo, several whistles sounded in the background. Then I noticed movement on the far side of the courtyard wall. Out of instinct, I immediately withdrew to the shadows to observe these new arrivals, these party crashers. Their identities were concealed behind black-hooded cloaks, but their gait told me they were female. What sort of mischief were they up to? Estates like this had been looted in the past for the priceless treasures lying about the premises. Artifacts collected throughout the centuries. But those raids were undertaken while the hosts were away. These individuals were in for quite a surprise. Yet as this thought crossed my mind, I sighted more movement from other areas of the courtyard. Then I realized that it wasn't a heist. It was an attack."

*****

Caliban was observing the festivities from the mezzanine. A small, pale hand reached over his shoulder and caressed his shirtless torso. He caressed the hand and brought it to his lips. Just as he was about to kiss the long-nailed fingertips, a deafening explosion rang out, and shards of the shattered front doors were sent flying across the room. Several pieces pierced the guests, and Caliban was thrown into the stairwell and knocked unconscious.

*****

"Self-preservation told me to leap the wall and make my escape, but kinship had me running toward the manor. Just as I neared the rear entrance, a distant explosion rang out, causing the ground to tremor, and the double French doors crashed open as a tangle of bodies burst through. Bodies that, only an instant ago, were tangled in the throes of passion were now in the throes of battle. The high-pitched screeches of vampires and the grunts and screams of humans quickly replaced the moans of ecstasy as the black-hooded assailants poured in from all sides.

"The battle raged throughout the entire property. There were fires blazing everywhere. It was fight or flight, so I chose flight. I darted for the courtyard wall before things could get worse, when I fell suddenly to my knees. Something had struck me from behind. I could feel the pain everywhere, even in my teeth. I glanced down and saw that there was a wooden arrow with a silver tip jutting out from my torso just below my heart, and it was causing my flesh to sizzle. In an instant I was back on my feet, facing the direction from where the arrow had come. In front of me, positioned on one knee and trying to load another arrow into an arcane crossbow amid the chaos, was a woman in a hooded cloak dressed in evening wear as if she were attending a dinner party. I couldn't help but see the humor in it. After all, it was a dinner party they were plundering.

"Once she noticed I was no longer incapacitated, she tossed aside the crossbow, rose to her feet, and was wielding what appeared to be a silver blade of ancient design. Her movements were almost as fluid as a vampire. 'Who are these mortals?' I asked myself. Holding the knife above her head, she screamed, 'Abomination, burn in hell!' Immediately I was within a hair's breadth of the woman with my fingers clenching her throat and gripping like a vise around the wrist of the knife-wielding hand. 'Who are you?' I asked.

"Her hood had fallen back, revealing dark hair and a shrewd face with thin eyebrows. The woman replied as best as one could while having their throat squeezed like a rotten tomato. 'We are the ones who will bring an end to your beastly existence. We are the—' *Squish.* And just like a rotten tomato, red flesh seeped through my fingers as she gargled on her own blood and her wrist snapped in two. In earnest, I had heard the ranting of these types before; besides, my time was limited, so I had to cut the conversation short.

"I leapt to the top of the courtyard wall and removed the arrow, but before flying off to freedom, I had to take one last look at the devastation. The damage was far worse than I had expected it to be. The manor was utterly in ruins. Shattered glass echoed like raindrops falling to the ground, and the once-aromatic gazebo was now fully aflame, offering only the stench of singed hair and seared flesh. How could a group of mortals, females at that, accomplish such damage? It was very upsetting.

"As I viewed the damage, thoughts of revenge raced across my mind. Who was responsible for this? And then there she was. Her hair was pulled back in a bun, and she was wearing a cloak and gown appropriate for the occasion: the infamous Lizzie Borden. I had never met her before, but I knew it was her, and that she was the cause of all that was happening.

"She was running from the manor toward a group of bodies that were crawling away from the now-cindering gazebo with the stumps of their legs on fire. One defiant torso turned over and glared at her with its one good silver eye. It was Caliban. His jet-black hair was now singed to his skull. She stopped short of the bodies and fired a plethora of arrows in each of them until they ceased clawing at the ground. Two other women joined her, and they searched the area for more survivors, or victims. Depending on your point of view. One of her companions discovered their friend's body some yards away with its throat ripped out.

"'We have a casualty, Ms. Borden,' she said. Her Irish accent was very heavy.

"Lizzie walked over to the Irishwoman to identify the person. She gave a short sigh of grief. 'Alice. She may have had her faults, but she had a kind soul,' she prayed. 'Gather what's left of her and put it in the carriage,' she ordered. 'Her parents deserve that much.'

"Another of the group ran upon the scene. She pulled her hood back, exposing bright auburn hair. 'The perimeter has been searched, and everyone has been exterminated,' she reported.

"'Excellent,' Lizzie relished. 'We need to leave this place now.'

"At first, I did not know if I heard her companion correctly. Everyone was exterminated? No. They were vampires. That couldn't be possible. Not all of them. Feelings of anger and loneliness began to well in my chest right above where the arrow had struck. A price had to be paid. Everyone else must die, I thought to myself. And that bitch will watch. Crouching atop the wall with fangs bared, I focused on the group, trying to decide which one would go first. It didn't matter as long as she died with them.

"However, I was so enthralled with my own ideas of revenge that I was not aware that I was leaning against one of the potted ferns lining the wall, my weight causing the plant to fall over to the ground and shatter. With feline reflexes, Ms. Borden and her cohorts quickly shot a look directly at my location. That was when our eyes met. And for a split second there was a look in her eyes. A look of anger, frustration, and desperation. It was a look I hadn't seen since. That was… until all this death started. It was the same look you humans had when you realized that the dead roaming the earth wasn't a dream, that moment when hope on the horizon was overcome and devoured by darkness." Varick said this while looking out toward the horizon and gesturing with his chin.

"However, that look quickly turned to fury when she reasoned what I was, and that not all the vampires had been dealt with. 'No, no, no!' screaming like a banshee, she began launching arrows and raining knives in my direction. I fell backward off the wall, feigning contact, and made my way to live another night. That was the last I saw of Lizzie Borden, and the last time I visited Massachusetts."

*****

"Nooo!" Lizzie was screaming at the top of her lungs while flinging arrows and knives at the top of the wall. The figure that was there a second ago had disappeared, but Lizzie swore that one of her knives rang true and hit the target. Her face was puffy with rage, and spit coated her mouth and chin. She felt someone gently grab her arm.

"We need to leave, remember." It was Maggie speaking in her comforting Irish tone. "We have to take care of Alice." Her eyes were filled with sympathy.

"Okay," Lizzie agreed. She started after the others but looked back one final time. "We'll meet again, you demon."

*****

"Wow. That was like…like watching a movie. Man, that was good," Henry complemented Varick.

Varick nodded slightly out of modesty and returned the compliment. "Thank you. It's nice to have an interested audience."

"It's not like I have anything else to do," Henry joked.

Varick gave one of his rare smiles.

"You know, there is one thing that bothered me, though," Henry expressed

"What was that?" Varick inquired.

"All of that history stuff you mentioned. I felt kinda dumb because I didn't know any of it. I never had a chance to learn any it," he said regretfully. "By the time I was old enough to go to school, all this dead shit started.

Varick remained silent as his intuition told him that Henry needed to speak.

"I was sitting in my grandma's living room watching *Heckle and Jeckle* cartoons while she was rolling tortillas in the kitchen." Henry went on. "Then the cartoons were interrupted by that message that looks like the beginning of *Outer Limits*. You know, where the TV screen scrambles with lines. Anyways, a voice came on and said that everybody should stay indoors. That's when my grandma came into the living room. She heard the same message on her radio. She started changing the TV channels until she found one airing the news. The anchorman was saying the same thing, but they were showing scenes from different cities where people were being chased by other people. The people being chased were scared shitless, and the ones chasing them seemed to be sick and fell every now and then.

"After viewing the footage, my grandmother shut off the television and went to her bedroom down the hall. When she returned to the living room, she locked the door and closed the windows, enforcing them with a piece of wood without saying a word.

"'Que paso, Abuela?' I asked her.

"'It's here, mi *hijo*. The three dark days and nights,' she told me, and then she pulled out a piece of white chalk from her apron pocket and started writing symbols on the corners of the door. You could only see the symbols when the light hit them from a certain angle. When she finished the inscriptions, she pulled a bag of salt out of the same apron pocket and sprinkled salt along the length of the windowpanes.

"'What is that for? I asked her.

"'It will keep the demons away, mi hijo,' she told me. 'Vente, it's time to pray.' She grabbed my hand and guided me to the altar of the Virgin Mary in the hallway where we knelt and prayed a rosary. It didn't work. None of it did."

Varick offered no comment. He only looked at Henry, thinking how difficult it must have been for a human to have their world turned upside down at such an early age.

Henry dabbed at his eye to stop a renegade tear. "Oh well," he said. "We have to get some shut-eye before we leave tonight." He grabbed a couple of tablecloths and his backpack and hopped onto the service counter to lie down. "Good night."

Varick walked to the back office and made himself comfortable on the old couch. "Good night, dear Henry."

CHAPTER 14

Two Birds with One Stone

The Dean was on one knee, peering through an eyelet from the old shoe, accompanied by so many children who knew not what to do. He watched the reception building with great interest and focus. The morning dew coated the foliage and sparkled like a field of diamonds in the sun's morning rays. Beneath the foliage squadrons of children surrounded the building on all sides, waiting with weapons, ready for the Dean's signal. Some held rusty knives and pickaxes, while others wielded clubs and short spears tipped with flint or salvaged iron. All he had to do was give the order, and they would all move as one like a well-organized colony of ants. Each one working toward the same goal.

If everything goes according to plan, he will be standing face-to-face with the next step in human evolution and the possible solution to the plague that allows the dead to regenerate by sunset.

The thought of the dead repulsed him. When the first reports surfaced describing the dead attacking innocent bystanders at bus stops and eating family members, many biologists and anthropologists considered the possibility that they were the next level in the human chain. But he knew better. This wasn't a George A. Romero movie where the dead can be trained, and they develop a sense of right from wrong. These beings with an extended life were the bane of humankind and its eventual demise. They were like cockroaches that needed to be exterminated, and Alistair Barrington, the Dean, may have found their poison.

*****

Timothy was peering as well. He was concealed in the bush with a dozen or so children under his command, never lifting an eye from their target. "What's takin' so damn long?" he said between gritted teeth. He lay on his stomach, anxiously tapping his thumb on the handle of the pickaxe he held in front of him. He glanced from side to side at the children he had personally assembled for the mission. The toughest kids in the Dean's family. He didn't want any scaredy-cats with him, and he definitely didn't want Frederick with him.

He squeezed the handle of the pickaxe until his knuckles turned white. He was ready for action. He was going to reach the building first, and then he was going to kill the man who stole food from their garden, and after this mission the Dean would make him his number one, which meant no more taking orders from Miss Smarty-Pants Gina. She'd be sent straight to the pit once he was in charge, along with that sissy Frederick. He smiled like a cat who just ate a very fat canary.

What is the Dean waiting for? he thought. It was getting hot under the bushes, and he was starting to get itchy.

*****

Frederick was lying next to Gina, nervously chewing on a twig. "You think the plan will work?" he said in between chomps. "What if they escape? What if the shadow kills us? What…?" He spoke rapidly without taking a breath, like someone about to have a panic attack.

Gina reached over and patted him on the shoulder. "Relax," she soothed him. "There's only two of them, and the Dean knows what he's doing. We just have to make sure to follow the plan. Okay?"

Frederick nodded in agreement while he chewed the twig to bits. At least Timothy wasn't with them. He was growing tired of Timothy's constant teasing and couldn't wait for him to be sent away on the journey.

Gina glanced at Frederick in sympathy and looked over his shoulders at the other children lying in wait with them. Each of them was just as nervous as Frederick, as was she, but she had to lead and that meant showing no fear. She just needed to wait for the call of the whistling duck and move forward. Timothy would lead more of the children in from the other side, and they would slowly enclose on the building.

She gulped down her fear, thinking of the shadow, and wondered if the plan was really possible. *Would they be able to capture it? And what about the friend?* She snapped out of it, feeling a little guilty at questioning the Dean's plan. He knew what he was doing. He was the smartest person in the world. She wiped beads of sweat from her forehead and looked at the sky. "Where's that signal? It's getting hot under here," she complained to herself.

*****

The Dean reached his arm out, and his attendees took his cup and placed a handkerchief in his hand. He wiped his hands and dabbed at the sweat on his upper lip. The temperature was rising rapidly, turning the inside of the minigolf shoe into a sauna. He looked out the shoe eyelet and saw that the sun was now high enough in the sky to glare down on the reception building unhindered by the surrounding forest. *Perfect*, he thought.

He turned on his knee and raised his hands upward as if he were about to offer a prayer. The children in the shoe looked up at him like little cherubs on the verge of taking flight. He looked every individual in the eye and called them by name. "Joshua, Damien, Ruth, etc." At the sound of their names, each raised their shoulders in confidence, boys and girls. All except Ruth, the cook who gazed upon the scene with skepticism.

After a short pause, he began to speak in a low whisper. "Follow the plan, and all will be well." Then he drew his hands to his mouth and gave the high-pitched whistle of the fulvous whistling duck.

*****

Varick was resting on the old sofa in the back office when he sensed movement. His eyes popped open, and he looked through the open door toward Henry in the customer-service area. He was sleeping soundly on the reception countertop covered with tablecloths. His head was resting on several soft rabbit furs bunched together like a pillow.

The movement was increasing and coming from all sides. Varick rose from the sofa and glided out to the center of the building.

"Henry," he stated calmly. "It appears we have to cut our nap short. Our mysterious hosts have decided to introduce themselves."

Henry sat up on the countertop rubbing his tired face when a crash sounded, and broken glass hit the floor, allowing a ray of sun to penetrate the building. Henry jumped from the counter, grabbed his spear from the floor, and took a position next to Varick with his machete in his other hand.

Another window shattered, and a bright sunbeam crossed in front of Varick. He took a step back to avoid its deadly ultraviolet rays.

Henry glanced down at the sunlit area in front of them and then to Varick. "Maybe we should've left yesterday."

About the Author

The author resides on the Big Island of Hawai'i, with his loving wife and beautiful children. He is a graduate of the University of Hawai'i at Manoa where he earned a degree in history as well as anthropology. He works as a case manager, servicing the mentally ill community. When he is not writing, he enjoys spending time with his family.

CPSIA information can be obtained
at www.ICGtesting.com
Printed in the USA
LVHW110816050822
725259LV00001B/81

9 781662 475412